SWEET ADDITIONS

A SWEET COVE MYSTERY BOOK 17

J. A. WHITING

For Amanda D.

Murdered July 2019, Worcester, MA
Strong and brave

I wrote the ending the way I wish it could be

1
_____

Angie Roseland and her twin sister, Jenna, sat in the living room of the Victorian mansion admiring all the gifts stacked in two corners of the room. Blue, pink, green, and yellow balloons decorated the space and vases of flowers had been placed on the side tables. The baby shower guests had just left and the four Roseland sisters, Jenna's husband, Tom, Angie's husband, Josh, and their family friend, Mr. Finch, relaxed in front of the fireplace before cleaning up. The family's two cats, Euclid, a big orange Maine coon, and Circe, a sweet, small black cat, rested on the rug by the fire. Snowflakes were gently falling outside the window.

"What a great time." Angie lifted her teacup to

her lips. "It was really wonderful. Thank you so much for hosting it."

Jenna agreed. "It was great to see everyone and you made such a terrific luncheon buffet."

Courtney, the youngest of the family, and Ellie, the middle sister, had put on a feast including homemade omelettes, waffles, home fries, fruit salad, calzones, sweet and tangy meatballs, ham and cheese rollups, individual tomato tarts, and mini mac and cheese cups. Angie, a baker, created a beautiful three-layer cake with pink, white, and blue frosting, and decorated it with ribbons and flowers made of marzipan. Jenna, a jewelry designer, made pretty bracelets for all of the guests as shower favors.

Euclid opened his mouth in a wide yawn before slowly blinking his green eyes and then placing his head on his paws.

"I'm tired, too, Euclid." Angie stifled a yawn of her own.

"I can't believe the babies will be here in a month," Courtney told them. "The time has flown by. I can't wait to meet Gigi, and Jenna's mystery baby."

Everyone knew that Angie and Josh were having a daughter, but Jenna and Tom didn't want to know what they were having, preferring a surprise.

"And both babies due within a week of each other." Mr. Finch rubbed his hand over the top of his cane. "It will be a happy day when the two new additions to our family arrive."

Circe looked to the man and meowed her approval.

While Finch and the sisters started to clean up, Josh and Tom began the task of moving the gifts out of the living room and into their homes. Angie and Josh lived in an apartment on one of the upper floors of the house and Tom and Jenna owned a house two doors down from the Victorian.

"We'll load the truck with your presents first and drive them over to the house," Josh suggested pulling on his coat.

"Then we can carry your gifts upstairs," Tom said. "You should put in an elevator one of these days."

"We'll put it on the list for the next renovation." Angie's blue eyes sparkled.

The Victorian had recently gone through some construction to add-on an apartment to the back of the house for Mr. Finch. Finch had owned a home whose property line abutted the Roselands' land, but he'd sold it to friends and the sisters added onto the Victorian so the older man would be close to them and would only need to leave his suite of rooms connected to the family room whenever he wanted to be with the family. Tom's construction company had handled the expansion and Finch now had a living room, kitchen-dining area, a four-season sunroom, a bedroom, and a bath. Finch and Courtney co-owned a popular candy store in the quaint center of Sweet Cove, a seaside town of stores, shops, restaurants, museums, and beautiful white-sand beaches on the North Shore of Massachusetts.

"Are you sure you two don't want to go have a nap?" Ellie asked. "Courtney, Mr. Finch, and I can handle this mess."

Jenna and Angie thanked their sister, but were willing and able to pitch in and started to clean off the buffet table in the dining room with Mr. Finch while Ellie and Courtney carried dishes to the kitchen.

Euclid and Circe jumped up on the China cabinet to watch the cleanup.

"I'm not sure I should bring this up," Finch said. "It may be nothing at all." He let his voice trail off.

Angie turned to the man. "You feel it, too?"

Finch looked relieved. "Ah. I should have known you were aware of the sensation, Miss Angie, but there's so much going on, I didn't want to say anything."

Jenna leaned against the dining table with a sigh. "I was hoping it was my imagination."

"Any ideas?" Finch asked the sisters.

"None." Angie pushed a strand of her dark blond hair behind her ear. "I've felt like I'm on pins and needles, a worried feeling washes over me every once in a while. I wish whatever it is, would leave us alone until after the babies are born."

"No such luck." When Jenna shook her head, her long brunette hair moved over her shoulders. Jenna and Angie were fraternal twins and did not share many physical characteristics. Angie was the oldest by a few minutes and looked more like Courtney, and Jenna was taller than her twin and had darker hair, but all the sisters shared the same big, blue eyes they'd inherited from their mother.

Courtney and Ellie returned to the dining room and when Courtney saw the look on the three family member's faces, she stopped in her tracks. "What's wrong with you?" Understanding quickly showed on her face. "Oh. I guess what I've been feeling the past few days hasn't been my imagination."

As Ellie stared at her siblings and Finch, her

shoulders dropped. "Oh, come on. Not now. Really? Something's going to happen now?"

"It seems so, Miss Ellie." Finch pushed his black-rimmed eyeglasses up the bridge of his nose as the cats let out howls from their perch on the cabinet.

The Roselands and Mr. Finch each had paranormal skills that they'd used to successfully assist the Sweet Cove police chief, Phillip Martin, in many crimes that had taken place in the area over the past two years.

Courtney, the one sister who loved her special abilities, rubbed her hands together. "Good. We haven't had a case in a few months. We're due, and I'm ready. Does anyone know what it's going to be about?"

The others shook their heads.

Ellie turned and headed for the kitchen. "I'll put coffee on. Chief Martin will be here in a few minutes."

Angie's eyes widened as she watched her sister leave the room. "She's doing it again."

One of Ellie's skills was her ability to know when someone was coming to the house. She always mentioned it in a nonchalant manner thinking that everyone else knew the person was on his or her way and that it had nothing to do with any paranormal talent. When the family pointed out that she was the only one who had any advance notice of an arriving friend or guest, Ellie always denied it.

The two cats released howls, and then the doorbell rang.

"Here we go." Jenna shook her head and went to open the front door.

"Hi, Jenna." Chief Martin stood on the porch. "When Lucille came home, I knew the baby shower was over. She had a great time. Sorry to come by right after the festivities, but I was wondering if I could talk to all of you about something." In his late-fifties, the police chief was tall and stocky and had a bit of gray showing at his temples. He and his wife, Lucille, were good friends with the Roselands and Finch ... and the sisters' grandmother, Virginia, who also had paranormal abilities, had worked with the police department for years in a *special* capacity before she passed away.

Courtney hurried over. "We knew something was up. Come on in. Ellie put coffee on."

"I didn't tell her I was coming." The chief's eyebrows went up, remembering Ellie's special skill. "Oh, right. I didn't need to tell her."

Angie greeted the man and took his coat. "Let's

sit at the dining table. There are lots of desserts left from the party."

When they were all settled around the table with coffee and dessert and had talked about how the baby shower went, Courtney addressed the chief. "Okay. Let's get on with it. What's wrong?"

"Nothing's wrong. Well, something is, but it's something odd, not exactly wrong. Although, I suppose it is," the chief beat around the bush.

"Has there been a murder?" Courtney asked.

"No." Chief Martin sat up straighter. "Nothing like that. There was a break-in."

"Where?" Angie questioned, feeling a prickly sensation run over her skin.

The chief set down his coffee mug. "Over at the nonprofit in Silver Cove."

"Brighter Days?" Ellie asked.

Euclid and Circe hissed.

Brighter Days was a community nonprofit organization that helped house and feed those in the area who were in need, assisted with health care costs, legal aid, and anything else that was warranted. The organization also taught personal finance classes for free to anyone who wanted to understand how to buy a home, save and invest, or get themselves out of debt. The organization was well-loved in the North Shore communities for its devotion to the residents and to the newly-arrived who needed a helping hand.

"Was money stolen?" Jenna's voice was tinged with worry. She'd volunteered with the organization in the past and knew that at times, there could be a quite a lot of money in the safe from donations that had come in.

"No, nothing was stolen." The chief shook his head.

"Vandalism?" Mr. Finch asked.

"No vandalism."

"What happened then?" Courtney asked the chief.

"Someone broke into the offices the other night and was caught on security tape."

"Have you arrested him?" Angie asked. "You know who he is since he's on the tapes?"

The chief shook his head. "He was wearing a mask."

Ellie groaned.

"He was wearing army fatigues, boots, the mask, a knitted hat, gloves. Not much of anything is showing that could be used to identify the person."

"If he didn't steal anything and he didn't

vandalize the place, what *did* he do?" Jenna questioned uneasily.

"He walked through the hallways and the offices, around and around, for about two hours," the chief revealed.

"Doing nothing?" Finch questioned.

"Just looking around."

"Two hours? Just looking at stuff?" Courtney asked. "What in the world was he doing that for?"

Chief Martin sighed. "Your guess is as good as mine."

2

The sisters and Mr. Finch bundled into their winter coats and drove in Ellie's van to the police station. Chief Martin led them to a small conference room where they gathered to watch the security video of the break-in at the Brighter Days Community nonprofit.

The black and white picture on the television screen looked foggy and unclear as they watched someone appear in the hallway and walk slowly past the doorways. The person opened the unlocked doors, looked inside the rooms for a few seconds, and then kept walking, in no hurry to make progress on his inspection of the spaces.

"I can't tell if it's a man or a woman." Courtney's eyes were pinned to the screen. "So I'm just going to call the person a *he*. He's nonchalant in his behavior. It's like he's strolling through the building, making his rounds like he's the security officer."

Chief Martin agreed. "The security footage has been copied to show the person in the different places he visited in the offices. There are several cameras positioned in different hallways and we've gathered the footage that shows the person moving through the non-profit."

The person had on a dark winter jacket, a dark knitted hat, a black mask that covered his entire face except his eyes, and he wore heavy boots and a pair of gloves. His lumbering gait made him seem awkward and uncoordinated.

"His clothing makes it impossible to see any identifying features." Angie gazed at the screen watching the person move through the hallways. "The fuzziness of the picture makes it hard to see the clothing in detail."

"It's creepy." Ellie voiced what everyone else was thinking. "He broke in and wandered around for two hours? Brighter Days isn't that big. He must have patrolled the hallways over and over."

"He did." Chief Martin nodded. "He looked into the offices from the hall, but never entered any of them. At least, none of the rooms that lead off the hallways that are seen on the tapes."

"What was he looking for?" Jenna wondered aloud.

"I don't know," the chief said. "He didn't leave the place carrying anything. He spent the entire time looking around."

"Was he familiarizing himself with the layout of the place?" Finch's index finger tapped his chin.

Chief Martin made eye contact with the older man. "The same thought occurred to me."

"Why though?" Courtney questioned. "For what purpose?"

"What goes on in the offices and rooms there?" Angie posed the question. "The activities at the non-profit could be a clue to what the intruder was looking for."

"Or," Jenna said ominously, "what he intends to do in the future."

A shiver ran over Angie's skin. "You think he might be planning something?"

"Why walk through the place for two hours unless you were looking for something or you were planning something?" Jenna asked.

"They hold fundraising events there," Ellie said. "I've been to a few of them."

"They hold language classes for new English-speakers. They offer different kinds of seminars like Buying Your First House, Saving and Investing, How to Pay for College, How to Manage Retirement, stuff like that," Jenna told them.

"They meet with people who need help with child care, who can't afford health services, who have lost their jobs and need help with retraining," Mr. Finch said.

"They do food drives and clothing drives, too," Ellie said. "There's also a small shop there selling used clothing and household items for very low prices. They do a lot of good for people."

"I don't like the idea that the intruder is casing the place," Jenna said. "He might be planning to make trouble."

"We're assigning an officer to be stationed daily at the non-profit for the next week," the chief said. "Unfortunately, we can't spare an officer any longer than that."

"Maybe the person will give up whatever he's planning to do when he sees a police officer is there during working hours," Finch said.

"I hope so." Chief Martin had a worried look on his face.

"Have you spoken with the employees and the

volunteers who work at Brighter Days?" Angie asked. "Did anyone mention a disgruntled worker?"

"We've spoken with them." Chief Martin fiddled with a spoon, twirling it between his fingers. "None of the workers have recently given notice and gone to other jobs. No one can remember anyone who seemed disgruntled, not an employee, not a volunteer, not a client. So far, there's no theory as to what the intruder wanted or why he entered the offices."

"The intruder might not have wanted anything at all," Ellie speculated. "He might not have even known what sort of office he was in. Maybe he only wanted the thrill of breaking and entering."

"If that's the case, that would be the best reason of all," Jenna said. "The person was only looking for a thrill, not to cause damage, not to steal anything, not to hurt anyone."

"Why dress like that though?" Angie asked. "He put a lot of thought and effort into his clothing. He made sure nothing about his features could be distinguished. He might have known there were working security cameras there. If he was looking just to break in for a thrill, would he have been so meticulous about disguising himself so well?"

"Could he have been looking for someone?" Finch asked. "Did he think the person he was searching for heard him enter the offices and hid somewhere? Was he walking around trying to flush out the person?"

Angie's eyes widened. "That's an awful thought."

"It scares me," Ellie said with an involuntary shake of her upper body. "It's like a horror movie."

"Can you rewind the tape?" Courtney asked the chief. "Is there any indication that the person is concealing a weapon?"

Everyone watched closely as the intruder once again walked the halls on the screen.

"It's hard to say," Chief Martin told them. "The jacket is bulky. He could easily have knives with him and a gun would be easy to hide under the heavy jacket."

"Maybe this is more ominous that we think," Jenna said. "Maybe the person's intention is much darker than we suspect."

"What about the person's age?" Finch asked. "Can we get a clue to the person's age by the way he moves?"

The group continued to watch the television.

"I don't think he's a teenager," Ellie said. "His movements aren't that quick or fluid. He has a lumbering gait, but that might be a put-on to throw off anyone who looks at this."

"How tall do you think he is?" Angie asked the chief. "Does the tape give any hints to the person's height?"

Chief Martin said, "It does. We walked through the halls of the non-profit and took measurements. We think the person is around five feet eight inches tall."

"That's something to go on," Angie said with forced optimism.

"The body movements don't suggest anything about the person's gender," Finch said. "And the clothing hides any details about the body shape. He could be thin or thick. There's no way to tell."

"So we don't know if the intruder is a man or a woman, we don't know if he's heavy or skinny, we don't know his age, and we have no idea of his motivation for breaking into the offices." Courtney shook her head. "This isn't going to be easy."

"Could the intruder have been looking for money?" Ellie asked. "Isn't there a safe in one of the rooms?"

"There is a safe in the first floor office," the chief said. "The business manager shares the office with the executor director and the technical manager. They're pinched for space so all the employees and volunteers share offices."

"Did anyone notice if the intruder lingered a little longer at any specific door?" Angie questioned.

Courtney said, "I noticed he stood at the threshold a little longer at a few offices, but the time he spent wasn't much different than at the other office doors."

"Could he have been looking for someone in particular?" Finch questioned.

"Are the names of the people who work in each of the rooms posted on the walls outside their offices?" Ellie asked.

Chief Martin zoomed in as best he could, but it caused the picture on the television to blur. "It looks like there might be names on the walls next to the doors."

"I can't make out what they say," Angie said. "It might be helpful to know who used the offices where the intruder stood looking in longer. It might give us an idea of who, if anyone, might be the person's target."

Chief Martin looked around the table at the Roselands and Mr. Finch. "Do any of you have the feeling that this was a break-in without cause ... that the intruder only wanted to experience the excitement of the breaking and entering? That there's nothing sinister behind it?"

No one spoke.

"I was afraid of that." The chief looked down with a sigh. "You all think there's more intent here than the simple exhilaration of breaking into a suite of offices?"

The family members nodded.

"Okay." The chief took in a long breath. "Can anyone accompany me to the Brighter Days offices tomorrow afternoon?"

"I'll go," Angie said.

"Me, too," Courtney answered. "I have the morning shift at the candy store and Mr. Finch is handling the afternoon so I can go with you after my shift."

"Thanks." The chief took out a pad of paper from the drawer of the old metal desk tucked in the corner of the room. "I'll go through the tapes a few more times and make note of which offices the intruder seemed to show more interest in. Tomorrow, we'll speak to the people who work in those particular offices."

"It's a good start." Angie sat tall in her seat. "We have a plan."

Chief Martin nodded to everyone around the table. "And that's more than we had when we came in here. We'll figure it out," he said encouragingly.

"We haven't been stumped by a case yet," Finch said with a smile. "And in the end, we'll triumph over this one as well."

Angie made eye contact with their adopted family member. *I hope you're right.*

3

The Brighter Days Community non-profit took up the first floor of an old brick building in the town of Silver Cove just north of Sweet Cove. There was a receptionist's desk in a small lobby inside the front door where two main hallways led to meeting rooms and offices.

"My office is down this way." Lydia Hendricks, the executive director, led Chief Martin, Angie, and Courtney to the hall on the right of the lobby. Fifty-year-old Lydia was tall and slender with blue eyes and chin-length dark blond hair. She wore slacks and a light blue suit jacket. "It's not really *my* office. I share it with two other people. Space is tight, but we don't want to spend the money to expand so we make do."

Leading the three investigators through an open door, they entered a cramped office with four desks, a safe off to the side, file cabinets, and a small meeting table. There was one window that let in some natural light which helped make the room seem a little bigger than it actually was.

Lydia introduced the other two women working in the office. "This is our business manager, Monica Windsor, and this is our tech manager, Bev Tarant."

Short and stocky, Monica was in her early forties and had chin-length brunette hair. She had a quick, friendly smile and a firm handshake.

Thirty-years old, Bev was around five feet seven inches tall, had a slim build, blue eyes, and shoulder-length blond hair. With a warm smile, she welcomed the visitors to the office.

There were three extra chairs arranged around the table and they all pulled the seats in close to talk.

"Do you know who the person is who broke in here?" Monica asked the chief. "Were you able to identify him?"

Chief Martin explained how little there was to work with. "Basically, the only thing we can say is the person is around five feet eight inches tall. The intruder was covered from head to toe, only the eyes were visible. We don't know for sure if the person is a man or a woman. We can't tell how old the person is either. There isn't much to go on. That's why we wanted to talk to the three of you."

"How can we help?" Lydia asked.

Angie told the office workers how the intruder seemed to linger a little longer in certain places in the hallways. "I'm calling the person a *him* for simplicity sake. He spent a little longer looking into this office than the others. We don't know if he was looking for something or someone, or was just getting a kick out of breaking and entering."

Courtney said, "He spent about two hours walking around in here. It's a long time to spend in a place if he was just looking for the excitement of breaking in. Our initial impression is that he was looking for something."

"But he didn't find it, I assume," Monica said.

"Nothing is missing, correct?" the chief asked.

Monica shook her head.

"Do some of the workers stay late sometimes?" Angie asked.

"Oh yes. We always have plenty to do," the director explained. "We all do more than what's in our job descriptions. Money is always tight. We can't hire more workers so we all do double-duty and jump in wherever we're needed. Some people stay late from time to time."

"The front door is locked after hours?" the chief asked. "Even if people are here working?"

"We lock the doors at 6pm," Monica said. "An identification pass is needed to come in after hours."

"Have there been any clients who might have caused some trouble here recently?" Chief Martin questioned.

The three women looked to one another and shook their heads.

"I don't know of any issues," Lydia said, and the other workers agreed.

"Some people who come in for help are frustrated and feeling depressed," Monica said. "They might be curt or impatient, annoyed, defeated, but after a short time, they understand we're here to help them and they relax."

"Has there been anyone in recently who has seemed more down than the usual client?" the chief asked.

"We can't think of anyone," Bev said.

Angie glanced at the unoccupied desk. "Are there four of you who share the office?"

The three women seemed to stiffen.

Lydia said, "There was a fourth woman until recently. She doesn't work here anymore."

Angie felt a wisp of nervousness in the air. "She went on to another opportunity?"

"We had to let her go. Joelle wasn't working out," Lydia said.

"What was her job?" Chief Martin asked.

"She was the bookkeeper and accountant." Lydia seemed to want to say more, but remained silent.

"I caught Joelle stealing from my purse," Bev said with a sigh. "She took some cash and a couple of credit cards from my wallet. She was hard to get along with. She was sullen a lot of the time. She took days off without informing anyone. Joelle could be secretive, she had an angry edge to her personality. It was really tense with her working here."

"Did you report the theft to the police?' the chief asked.

"We didn't," Lydia said. "There are some discrepancies with the books. Another accountant is doing an audit. If something comes up, then we'll have to report her to law enforcement."

"You think she stole from the non-profit?" Angie asked.

"It's an unfortunate possibility," Lydia admitted.

"We didn't want to bring it up since we don't have the necessary proof."

Chief Martin nodded. "We'd like to interview each of you individually. It shouldn't take long."

Bev remained while Lydia and Monica left the room to work elsewhere until it was their turn to be interviewed.

"How long have you worked here?" Angie used a pleasant tone of voice to put the woman at ease.

"A little over two years," Bev said. "I love the job. My co-workers are great. We get along well, which is a good thing since the room isn't exactly large." She smiled and gestured at the tight quarters.

"You handle the technology needs?" Courtney questioned.

"That's right. The network, the desktops, the laptops, printers, the website ... any issues that come up. There's always something to do." Bev nodded. "There's always something that's got a glitch or someone doesn't understand how to use the software. Things like that."

"Did you grow up in the area?" Angie asked.

"In Gloucester." Bev chuckled. "I didn't get far, did I? I live here in Silver Cove, only twenty minutes from my family."

"Are you married?"

"I'm not. I recently stopped dating someone I'd been seeing. I'd like to find a permanent partner someday, but so far I haven't had any luck."

Angie's mental radar buzzed when Bev said she'd stopped seeing someone. "Was the break-up amicable?"

Bev sighed. "Allen thought we should continue to date, but I knew there wasn't any point. We were too different. Our personalities didn't mesh that well. He agreed that moving on was the right thing to do even if it was hard to accept."

"How long had you been together?"

"Not long. Four months."

"Have you had any trouble with anyone recently?" the chief asked. "An argument, a fender-bender, a disagreement?"

"No. Everything's the same as always." Bev's eyes widened and her shoulders tensed. "Do you think the intruder is targeting one of us?"

Chief Martin didn't want to alarm the young woman. "We don't have any reason to believe so. We're just covering all the bases. These questions are simply normal procedure."

Bev seemed to relax a little. "I see."

Monica Windsor was the next one to speak with

the investigators and she came in and sat down in her office chair when Bev left the room.

The same set of questions was asked. Monica grew up in New Hampshire and went to college in Boston. She'd worked for various non-profits over the years, and had been at Brighter Days for the last six years. She enjoyed her co-workers, was married, had two small children, and loved to bake.

"Any run-ins with anyone recently?" Courtney questioned. "Is there anyone who is angry with you or annoyed with you?"

Monica kidded, "You mean besides my husband and kids?" She laughed. "No, there's nothing like that. If someone is angry with me, I haven't had time to notice."

Lydia came in to be interviewed and had much the same things to say. She'd always wanted to work in non-profits, she graduated from Cornell, went to school for her MBA, and began her career at a small non-profit, had been working at Brighter Days for ten years, she lived in Silver Cove, and she did a good deal of volunteer work as well as serving on two boards of directors. "I can't think of anyone who has given the workers a bit of trouble. Everything has been running smoothly here."

The chief asked, "Can you give us a description of Joelle Young?"

Lydia said, "Joelle is thirty. She was in the Army for several years and served overseas. She has short blond hair. She has a stocky build. Joelle works out a lot, lifting weights, running. She's strong and muscular. She received her bachelor's degree in math from the University of Pennsylvania."

"How tall would you say she is?"

"Oh, let's see. Five feet seven?"

"Is she still in the area?"

"I'm not sure where she is," Lydia said.

"Single? Married? A family?" the chief asked.

Joelle is single, no kids. She told us she has some family in Washington state. She never talked about them. She was close-lipped about her life outside of work."

"Are you married?" Angie asked.

"My husband and I divorced a year ago. We have two sons, they're in their late twenties. We'd grown apart. We both wanted to head in different directions," Lydia said.

"Did you initiate the split?" the chief asked.

Lydia sighed. "I did, yes, but my husband had cheated on me so he was the one who actually led us down the path to dissolving the marriage. I wouldn't stay with him after that. I could never trust him again."

"Does he live in the area?" Courtney asked.

"He lives in Newburyport."

"Are you in touch?"

Lydia shrugged. "I'd prefer not to be, but yes, he gets in touch. His fling didn't work out and he wants to get back together. That isn't going to happen."

"How is your ex-husband taking that?" Chief Martin asked.

"Not that well. He should have thought things through before he acted." Lydia shrugged, and then she looked the chief in the eye. "You aren't thinking that Roger is the one who broke in here? It's not him. He would never do anything of the sort. He wouldn't do anything illegal. He's a corporate attorney. Roger would never do anything to jeopardize his legal career."

"Do you know if anyone working here is having trouble with someone outside of the office?" Angie asked.

"I can't think of anyone." Lydia took in a long breath. "Did Bev mention her recent break-up?"

"She did," the chief said.

"The man she was seeing wanted to keep dating and it was hard for him to hear that Bev wanted to end the relationship, but he was understanding about how she felt. Did she tell you this?"

"Bev told us she was the one to end the relationship," Chief Martin said. "She told us the man didn't want to stop seeing her, but that it was amicable when they went their separate ways."

"That's true. Allen called Bev a lot at first just to talk or ask her for advice about things. After a while, Bev told him she didn't think it was a good idea to talk so often. She thought it would just extend the time it took for them to move on," Lydia told them.

"How did he handle her suggestion?" Courtney asked.

"He reluctantly agreed and they don't communicate anymore." Lydia shook her head. "I wish my ex-husband would be mature like Allen and accept that things aren't going to work out. Roger just can't get it through his head that I'm not getting back with him. I guess he thinks if he badgers me enough, I'll change my mind."

A flush of nervousness ran over Angie's skin and she protectively placed both of her hands over her abdomen.

4

Snow gently fell outside the windows of the Sweet Dreams Bake Shop where Angie was closing up for the day running the dishwasher and preparing some items for the next day's business. Mr. Finch and Orla Abel sat at the counter drinking coffee and chatting with Angie. Orla and her husband, Mel, were friends of the family and had moved to Sweet Cove after meeting each other at the bed and breakfast inn Ellie ran out of the Victorian. When Jenna's and Angie's babies arrive, Orla and Mr. Finch would be taking care of the children while the mothers worked.

"Why is it snowing all the time?" Orla shook her head. "We just get the driveway and sidewalks cleared and another few inches come down and we need to shovel again."

"It's been an unusually cold and snowy winter," Finch pointed out. "Why not hire the man I hired to plow and shovel?"

"I think we should."

Orla and Mel had recently purchased Mr. Finch's house which shared a property line with the Victorian. Finch had been in his new suite of rooms for a couple of weeks and loved living in the new addition to the mansion.

"I'm thankful not to have to walk over here in the snow anymore," Finch smiled. "I just open my door and I step into the family room. And my apartment is perfect, so spacious and open."

"It's great having you in the house." Angie put some clean dishes on the shelf in the cabinet. "If you need us for anything, we're all just a shout away."

"And when the babies come, I'm here when you need me." Finch set his cup on the saucer. "How is Louisa doing at the museum bake shop?"

"She's a pro. I don't know what I'd do without her." Angie pressed the button to start the dishwasher.

Angie's friend and employee, Louisa, was

helping to manage the two bake shops Angie owned, one located in the Victorian, and the other at the Sweet Cove museum. Louisa and Angie took turns working at each location and met daily to talk about any issues that had come up. The young women worked well together and the opportunity was one Louisa was grateful for.

When Orla left the bake shop to meet her husband in town for dinner, Mr. Finch asked what Angie thought about the meeting at Brighter Days that day.

Angie pushed a honey blond strand of hair behind her ear. "I got the strangest feeling when we were talking to the non-profit's director about her ex-husband. He cheated, the couple got divorced, and now the man is asking to get back together. The conversation made me feel unsafe as if I had to protect my baby from the situation."

"You sensed some danger?" Finch's eyes darkened.

"I guess. I'm not sure. I felt uneasy, but maybe it's just some hormonal thing that has me jittery."

"How did you feel when you were at the non-profit looking around?"

Angie's forehead furrowed in thought. "When we

were walking around, I didn't pick up on anything about the intruder. The anxious feelings started while we were talking with the director."

"No one at the business had any idea who the intruder might be?" Finch asked.

Angie shrugged. "They seemed baffled by the intrusion and had no guesses about who might want to break into the offices."

Finch rubbed his chin. "I suppose it could have been random."

"Someone dressed up in camouflage clothes, a hat, and a mask and went out looking for someplace to break into?"

"I think the place was chosen ahead of time," Finch explained. "But the choice may have been random. The intruder may not have any link to Brighter Days. He may not have any link to anyone who works there or goes there looking for assistance."

"That will make finding him more difficult." Angie wiped down the counter.

"I worry that the intruder isn't done with his exploits," Finch said.

"You think he'll go back? Do you think he'll escalate somehow?" A shiver ran over Angie's skin.

"I don't think breaking in and walking around will be satisfying enough. It may have given him an initial thrill, but he'll need to do something more to get any new gratification."

Angie's blue eyes were pinned on her friend. "Do you think his real intention is to hurt someone?"

Finch didn't answer right away. "I hope I'm wrong, but it is the feeling I get. Are you going to return to Brighter Days to speak further with the employees?"

With a nod, Angie said, "We're going back on Thursday. Would you be able to come?"

"I'd like to go with you and Chief Martin. Perhaps another pair of eyes and ears would be helpful. You know how some people like to open up to an old man." Finch winked.

Angie chuckled. "It's not your age that makes people enjoy speaking with you, Mr. Finch. It's your warm personality."

"Actually, Miss Angie, I think it *is* my age. People think they can tell me things because I won't be around long enough to reveal their secrets."

Angie cocked her head to the side. "Well, they'd be wrong if they think that. Something tells me you're going to be around for a very, very long time."

Josh and Angie stood together folding the new baby clothes and placing them in the dresser drawers. They'd already unpacked the car seat, the stroller, the playpen, and the two highchairs, one for their apartment and one for the kitchen downstairs.

Euclid and Circe sat next to the crib watching the activity.

"I can't believe all the gifts we got from the baby shower," Josh said. "Everyone was so generous."

Angie handed her husband a soft, pink and lavender blanket to put away on the closet shelf. "It's a huge help to get all of these things."

After putting the gifts away and with the cats following behind them, the couple went to their kitchen to make some tea.

Josh asked if Angie needed to take some time off from work before the baby arrived. "Gigi will be here in a few weeks. You have Louisa and the other employees. You can afford to work less."

"I love the bake shops. If I didn't go into work, I'd get lazy. It's good for me to be on my feet and move around. If I get tired, I'll take a day off." Angie poured the hot water into the mugs and she and Josh went to cuddle together on the sofa where she filled him in on the trip to Brighter Days.

Euclid and Circe jumped up on the sofa to join them.

"I don't like the sound of this." Josh put his arm around his wife's shoulders. "I'm glad Mr. Finch will go with you on Thursday. He might be able to sense something."

One of Finch's skills was being able to perceive something about a person by touching him or her, shaking a hand, or holding onto an object at the same time.

"People tend to open up to Mr. Finch so someone might say something that will help us figure out who the intruder is and what he wants." Angie blew on her tea and pulled a soft blanket over her knees. Circe gently pressed her front paws against the blanket and began to purr.

"Mr. Finch thinks things might escalate with the intruder," Angie said, running her hand over the black cat's silky fur.

Josh shifted on the sofa to better see his wife's face. "Do *you* think so?"

Angie gave a little nod. "I don't think the intruder is going to stop at one break-in. Maybe next time, he'll break in at a different place of business or at a store, but I have a feeling he has some connection to Brighter Days."

"Could he be a former employee?" Josh asked as Euclid moved onto his lap.

"Possibly, or he has a connection to someone who works there or to someone who goes there for assistance."

"Did you get a sense of the intruder's mood when you watched the security tapes?"

Angie blew out a long breath. "The intruder stood at a few of the doorways longer than at others. There was something subtle about how he held his body that made me think his muscles were tensing, like he was angry or upset. Sometimes, he seemed to move with purpose, other times, he seemed content to stroll around like he was early for a meeting and was waiting for someone to show up. These were just my impressions. I might be completely off-base."

"Has anyone at Brighter Days had an argument with someone recently?" Josh scratched the orange cat's cheeks.

Angie said, "The director, Lydia Hendricks, and her husband, Roger, divorced about a year ago. She told us her ex-husband has asked for forgiveness and wants to get back together with her, but she isn't open to the idea and refuses to do so. I felt cold and uneasy when Lydia talked about him, but she's adamant that her ex-husband is not the man who broke into the offices. Her ex-husband is a corporate attorney and Lydia is sure he would never do anything to ruin his career."

"Will Chief Martin speak to Roger Hendricks?"

"He will. The chief wants to know where Hendricks was during the time the person broke into Brighter Days."

"What about a security guard? Will the non-profit hire someone to be on-site during the night?" Josh asked.

"They can't afford to hire a security guard, but police officers will ride by during the night watching for any signs that someone has broken in again," Angie said.

"Is there an alarm on the place? Did the person know how to circumvent an alarm?"

"There isn't an alarm," Angie told Josh. "They lock the doors at 6pm and anyone who wants to go into the offices after that has to use an identification badge to swipe themselves in and out."

Josh took a swallow from his mug and set it down on the coffee table. "Do you think the intruder will return to the non-profit and break-in again?" Josh asked.

"I think he will." Angie's voice was soft. "This isn't over. It wasn't a one-time thing. He'll return. I'm sure of it."

Euclid lifted his head and let out a long, deep hiss.

5

It was a biting cold morning when Mr. Finch, Angie, and Jenna arrived at Brighter Days before the non-profit opened for the day and they met Chief Martin in the parking lot. The chief had called them at 7am to ask if they could come to Silver Cove as soon as they could, and on the drive over, the three of them had speculated about what might have happened.

"What's wrong? Did the intruder return?" Having left her gloves at home, Angie rubbed her hands together to ward off the cold.

Mr. Finch held onto Jenna's arm and clutched his cane in one hand as they hurried over to listen to Chief Martin.

"He broke in again last night. The time stamp on the security tape puts his visit at around 3 - 4 am.

The officers rode by at midnight, 2am, and 5am. I wouldn't be surprised if the intruder knew when the officers made their passes by the building." Chief Martin shook his head.

Jenna, Angie, and Finch were visibly shivering.

"Let's go inside and get out of this cold." The chief led them into the offices. "Lydia Hendricks came into work early today, a little after 6am. She has an important presentation coming up and wanted some quiet time alone in the office to do some preparation."

"What did she find when she arrived?" Jenna asked, a little afraid to hear the answer.

"I'll show you."

In the lobby and the reception area, two officers were checking around the desks and chairs as the chief walked by, nodded, and took his guests down the hallway to the office he and Angie were in the other day.

Chief Martin paused at the doorway. "Go in and have a look."

Angie gave him a look of worry, but he just nodded and said, "It's okay. It's just a couple of objects."

Angie was the first to step into the room and at first, she didn't notice anything amiss. Then she saw the things, and her heart jumped into her throat.

"Oh," was all Jenna said when she spotted two items on Bev Tarant's desk.

Finch came in and followed the young women's gazes. "Oh, my."

Two objects had been left on the top of Bev's scuffed wooden desk. A pair of handcuffs and a single bullet.

The chief moved into the office. "Our intruder left a calling card. Well, two calling cards."

"When Lydia came in, she found them?" Angie asked, her voice sounding tight.

Chief Martin gave a nod. "She ran out to her car and called the police station. She was scared to death. She was afraid the intruder might still be in the offices."

"I can see why she was frightened." Jenna turned her attention back to the objects.

"Where is Ms. Lydia now?" Finch asked.

"She was taken down to the station. She told me she needed some time to collect herself. A detective is speaking with her. She'll be back shortly. I asked the investigators to give us twenty minutes or so in here. Maybe you can look around. See if ... you know ... if you can sense anything."

"Before we do that," Angie said, "can you tell us what's on the security tape?"

"The intruder walked down the hallway. He's dressed as he was before, baggy camouflage pants, work boots, a heavy, bulky jacket, gloves, knit hat, sunglasses, and a scarf covering the lower face. He paused at the door to the office, stared into the room, then stepped in. The security system only shows the halls, not the offices themselves. We couldn't see him when he was in here. He came back out about five minutes later. We assume he left the items on the desk. He walked away down the hall and then left the building."

"A bullet and handcuffs," Angie said softly. "A threat. A lethal threat."

"Aimed at Bev Tarant, the tech manager?" Jenna asked.

Chief Martin said, "That's the assumption, however, you know how assumptions sometimes go. Maybe the intruder wanted to frighten one person in particular who works in this room. He chose a desk and placed the things on it. He might not know which desk belongs to who, so he left the things on one of the desks for the women to find when they came in to work."

"Was the plan to scare all of them ... or only one of them?" Finch asked.

"Unknown," Chief Martin admitted. "Shall I leave you for a few minutes to see what you can sense?"

The three amateur sleuths nodded, the chief stepped away, and they moved slowly around the cramped space. After a few minutes of standing and looking at the things in the room, Angie sat in Bev's chair, Finch took Lydia's seat, and Jenna sat at Monica's desk. They remained silent and tried to open themselves to anything that floated on the air.

Angie could feel Gigi kicking and she placed her hand on her abdomen, then closed her eyes and took deep breaths. Lights flashed behind her eyelids and her body flooded with anxiety and an urge to run from the room.

A soft tapping came from the doorjamb, and Angie turned to see the chief.

"Sorry to disturb you, but the investigators need to get back in here."

Surprised that the time was up already, Angie felt a little woozy when she stood, but she collected herself and followed the others out into the hall. The chief brought them to a small empty office space.

"Anything?" he asked.

Angie pushed her hair back from her face. "I felt nervous. I felt like I needed to get away, to escape from the room."

"I sensed anger," Jenna said, "but also an arrogance, a smugness, a mean intention."

The chief looked to Mr. Finch.

"I had similar sensations, a desire to get away, an arrogant, dangerous, unsettled presence." Finch stroked his chin. "Is it possible for me to touch the things the intruder left behind?"

"That's a great idea, but we'll have to do it another day. The investigators have the top priority. If there's something for you to sense from the objects, will a day or two cause the ... whatever it is you pick up on ... to dissipate? Will you still be able to sense what was there?" Chief Martin was always unsure how to phrase things when he spoke of the paranormal with the Roselands and Mr. Finch.

"Sensations will probably linger here for one or two days," Finch said.

"I'll get you in as soon as possible," the chief said. "Could any one of you tell who the items were meant for?"

"I was sitting the closest to the handcuffs and the bullet," Angie said. "I could feel a powerful energy coming from them ... it made me want to run."

"I couldn't tell who the message was for," Jenna said. "But I could feel the negative energy from the objects. They made me feel antsy, anxious."

Finch rubbed the palm of his hand over the top of his cane. "I felt anger. I could feel a person's need to teach someone a lesson. The room was flooded with ill intent."

"Amazing." The chief nodded. "Could you tell if the intruder was male or female?"

Finch said, "I believe it is a man. There was a musky smell in the room, probably coming from a male energy, a heated anger, but that odor can also come from a woman."

Chief Martin played the security tape for them, and when it was over, their eyes were wide.

The intruder had a baseball bat and as he strolled down the hall, he checked the doors to see if they were locked. If the door was locked, the man smashed it with the bat until the lock popped, then he moved to the next door. If a door was unlocked, he would enter the room for a minute or two. During that time, he used the bat to break something in the office.

"Odd," Jenna said. "If a door was locked, he hit until it opened, but he didn't go into those rooms. He only went into the rooms that were unlocked."

"And broke something in the offices that were unlocked," Finch pointed out.

Angie asked the chief what the intruder's behavior might mean.

"I have no idea. A psychologist will be consulted for an opinion," the chief told them.

"What did he break in the offices?" Angie asked.

The chief said, "Whatever caught his eye, a laptop, a framed photo, a calculator, a lamp. He only broke one thing in each of the rooms he went into."

"It's orderly," Angie suggested. "He must have had a reason for what he did. In a way, his anger was restrained, controlled."

"That's true, Miss Angie," Finch said. "You make a keen observation."

"If the man broke in around 3am, he wasn't expecting to run into any of the workers," Jenna said. "So his visit was meant to send a message of some kind, not to hurt anyone."

Finch asked, "What time was it when the first break-in took place?"

"Between 7:30pm and 9:30pm."

"The man may have hoped to run into someone who was working late that evening," Finch observed. "But this time, he came when he knew no one would be working in here. Two different intentions, perhaps."

"Good thinking, Mr. Finch," Angie said.

"The first time, he was observing," Chief Martin said. "This time he left a message."

"But what *is* the message?" Angie asked.

"That someone who comes into these offices is in trouble. Most likely it's one of the people who uses the office where he left the bullet," the chief suggested.

A feeling of dread washed over Angie and a sense of weakness invaded her muscles. "Why? What's the reason one of them is in trouble?"

Chief Martin looked fatigued with a few deep wrinkles showing around his eyes. "That's one of the things we're going to find out, but the first thing we need to discover is *who*. Who is the intruder and who is the intruder's intended victim?" The chief took in a deep breath. "And we'd better be quick about it."

6

In his late fifties, Roger Hendricks worked as a corporate attorney and was a partner at a multi-national firm outside of Boston. His office had walls of fine wood and the gleaming wood floors were covered with expensive handmade rugs in muted colors. The wall behind his massive desk was all glass providing spectacular views of the ocean.

Tanned, trim and fit, Hendricks was wearing a stylish gray suit when he welcomed Chief Martin and Angie into the office.

"I'm sorry to hear that Brighter Days is dealing with break-ins." Roger took a club chair while Angie and the chief sat down on the sofa. "Any idea who is responsible?"

"It's being investigated," Chief Martin said. "We'll know more in a few days."

"How is Lydia holding up? Is she doing okay?" Roger clasped his hands together and rested his elbows on the arms of the chair.

"She seems to be dealing well with the intrusions," Angie explained. "She is unruffled, she's reassuring to the workers, and she's taking care of business as usual."

"Good for her. Lydia has always been a strong, focused person." Roger nodded. "Do you think the intruder is someone local to the Sweet Cove and Silver Cove areas?"

"That's being looked at." Chief Martin kept the details close and he had no intention of sharing important information about the case. "Do you live in the Boston suburbs?"

"I live in Newburyport. I take the train back and forth."

"Lydia told us you travel quite a bit for work," the chief said. "Have you been away recently?"

"I haven't." One of Roger's eyebrows went up and he rested a steely gaze on the police chief. "You certainly don't suspect me, do you?"

The chief said, "We're speaking with friends and relatives of the Brighter Days workers. It's all customary procedure. It's vital to know the connections between people, where people were on the evenings of the break-ins, and what they might know about anyone associated with Brighter Days who might recently be disgruntled over something."

"You're aware that Lydia and I are divorced, correct?" Roger asked.

"Yes, we know that," Angie replied. "The two of you still speak though?"

"On occasion." Roger's face looked a little tense.

"Would you describe your relationship as amicable?"

"Yes, I would." Roger shifted in his chair, his forehead furrowing slightly.

"Could you tell us where you were on the evening of the first break-in?" Chief Martin asked.

Roger bristled. "I was in Newburyport. At home."

"Were you alone?"

The man let out a sigh. "I was alone. I picked up a takeout meal from an Italian restaurant that I pass as I drive home from the commuter rail parking lot. I had work to do and I needed to get to it right away, so I decided to get dinner to take home. I was at home for the rest of the night."

"When was the last time you saw Lydia?"

Roger ran his hand over the top of his thinning

hair. "Oh, let's see. It's been a while, maybe four months ago? We had some papers to sign."

"But you've spoken since then?"

"A few times."

"Has she spoken with you since the break-ins?"

"No. When I heard about the incident, I texted her, but she hasn't responded. I'm sure she's very busy with everything," Roger said.

Chief Martin asked, "Is there a chance you and Lydia might get back together?"

Roger's eyes widened. "Why are you asking that?"

"We wonder about the state of your relationship," the chief said. "Are the two of you working to reconnect?"

Roger looked like he was going to spit. "I don't see what that has to do with the Brighter Days case."

"It could have something to do with the case." The chief's voice was firm. "Law enforcement is looking at every angle."

Roger didn't answer the question he was asked, instead he sat in his chair with a look of anger on his face.

"Would you like to get back together with Lydia?" Angie asked gently.

"I don't know. Does Lydia have anything to say about that?"

Chief Martin said, "We haven't asked her yet." It wasn't a lie because the reality was that the chief didn't have to ask Lydia about the topic since she freely offered her opinion that her marriage was over and had no interest in rekindling anything with her ex-husband.

"Have you heard any details about the intruder's second visit to Brighter Days?" Angie asked.

"A few things. Not many. I heard he broke a few things during the second break-in. The first time, he just looked around and didn't do any damage." Roger's expression was serious. "He was in the offices for two hours the first time? What was he actually doing? He couldn't have been just walking around looking at things for two hours. Did he want to get caught? Is that why he lingered in there? Is that why he came back the second time?"

"We're not sure of the reason," the chief said. "More light will be shed on things as the investigation goes on."

"What else have you heard about the break-in?" Angie wanted to see if Roger might mention the items that had been placed on Bev Tarant's desk.

"Just what was in the news. Lydia certainly hasn't

shared any inside information with me." Roger pressed his back against the chair.

"Do you know Lydia's office mates?" the chief asked. "Monica Windsor or Bev Tarant?"

"I've met them, sure. There were always events to go to for the non-profit, fundraisers, community events, things like that. Bev and Monica were always there."

"Do you get along well with them?" Chief Martin asked.

"Sure, they're nice people."

"Would you say you know them well?"

"No, not well. They're casual acquaintances."

"Do you know anything about their lives outside of work?"

"No, I don't. Only that Monica is married and has kids. Bev is younger. I believe she was dating someone, but I'm not sure. I don't remember exactly."

Angie asked, "Is there anyone who works at Brighter Days you would consider odd or a nuisance? Maybe Lydia spoke about someone who was a bother?"

Roger's brow furrowed. "There was a custodian who wasn't doing a good job, but I don't think Lydia had to do anything about it. I recall he left work one day and didn't return."

"How was he a bother?"

"He could be surly. He didn't do a good job. Sometimes, he wouldn't show up for work and didn't call to say he'd be out. That's all I remember."

"Do you recall the man's name?" Angie asked.

"I don't. Ask Lydia. She'll know."

Chief Martin nodded. "How about the clients? Were any of the clients causing issues?"

"There were just little things," Roger said. "Some clients were demanding and ungrateful. Some could be mouthy, you know, always complaining, others being rude. Lydia always said it was a result of a lot of stress in the client's life. I'm not in frequent contact with Lydia so I can't speak about anyone who has been a problem recently."

"Did you ever worry about your wife's safety at work?"

Roger pondered the question. "Not really. Any issue that came up was handled quickly. No one ever threatened Lydia or her workers. She never told me she was afraid to go to work. There are clients who are addicted to drugs who go to Brighter Days for help, but they never caused any problems. I wouldn't know about anything recent." The man looked at the chief. "Why do you think this guy has targeted the non-profit?"

"It could be random," the chief said.

"Have other non-profits in the area been targeted?" Roger asked.

"Not that we know of," Chief Martin said. "Just Brighter Days."

"The guy must be a nut or a troublemaker. Most likely, he's been in trouble before."

Angie used a soft, non-challenging tone of voice when she asked, "Would you mind sharing with us what sparked your divorce?"

Roger's eyes narrowed and he looked like he might speak sharply at the young woman across from him. "I do mind sharing. Ask Lydia. I'm sure she'd love to tell you what a rotten person I am."

"Is that what she'll say to us?" Angie asked.

"Most likely. Lydia isn't exactly a forgiving person." Roger adjusted the perfect white cuff of his shirt.

"Do you think all transgressions should be forgiven?" Angie asked gently.

"I suppose not, but I think it damages a person when they hold onto hurt and won't let it go."

"Is that what Lydia is doing?" Angie wanted to hear more from Roger about his and Lydia's break-up. She wanted to know if he harbored ill will towards his ex-wife and if he did, what would he do to get back at her?

"You'll have to ask Lydia about that. I can't read her mind."

"Do you own a gun?" Chief Martin asked.

Roger's head turned quickly to the chief. "A gun? Why do you ask?"

"It's a question that we ask when we do interviews," the chief said. "We ask everyone the same types of things."

"If I owned a gun, there would be paperwork filed with the town. Why don't you check with them?" Roger's gaze was steely. "There's no point in my answering the question. I could lie about it. If you want to know the truth, it would be better for you to look it up."

"I would still like to hear your answer," the chief told the attorney.

Roger stared at the chief for several seconds, a little muscle twitching at the side of his jaw. "I don't own a gun. I've never had any interest in owning a gun. If I ever need protection, I'll hire someone who is a heck of a lot better shot than I could ever be."

7

Wearing a blue apron, Angie stood at the kitchen counter and used the mixer to cream the butter and sugar in the big glass bowl. Euclid and Circe watched from on top of the refrigerator.

"We didn't get much out of Lydia's ex-husband," Angie told Jenna and Mr. Finch. "He told us little things he knew about from before they got divorced. He said Lydia wasn't very forgiving and she shouldn't hold on to hurt."

Jenna rolled her eyes as she lifted the teacup to her lips. "Hurt caused by him. Lydia should forgive him so he can go out and cheat on her again? What about accepting the consequences of your actions and not blaming Lydia for reacting to your bad behavior?"

"Exactly," said Mr. Finch.

Euclid hissed from his perch.

"Roger didn't like the personal questions Chief Martin asked him." Angie used a spatula to scrape the butter and sugar mixture from the sides of the bowl. "He bristled at some of them. Yes, the questions can be difficult, but law enforcement is trying to solve a crime to keep people safe. The point isn't to protect some people from embarrassing questions, it's to find a criminal who seems to be escalating in dangerousness."

"Did Roger seem like he could be the intruder?" Jenna asked. "Was there anything about him that might suggest he was the one who broke into the non-profit?"

"I didn't get a feeling from him one way or the other." Angie added some vanilla extract to the bowl. "Roger said he was at home when the break-in occurred, and he was alone so there isn't anyone who can vouch for him."

"If Roger is planning to hurt Lydia," Mr. Finch said, "he might have placed the handcuffs and the bullet on Bev's desk to throw off the investigators. Let the police think that Bev is the intended victim of whatever he plans to do, when in reality, Lydia is the one he's threatening."

Angie paused from her baking. "That's good thinking. And even if Roger isn't the intruder, the actual criminal may have done the same thing ... leaving the bullet and the handcuffs on Bev's desk to make the police think it's Bev who is the future victim."

"But why allude to a future crime?" Jenna asked. "Why leave a bullet on anyone's desk? Why give the police advance notice that you're planning to hurt someone?"

"I think it's a game of cat and mouse," Angie explained. "The criminal is taunting the police. He's bold in planning the crime and he's confidant in his ability to elude law enforcement."

"In short, he is thumbing his nose at the police," Finch said.

Jenna asked, "Do you think the intruder is threatening Bev, or is Bev the decoy?"

"I don't know," Angie said. "When we were in the office, I felt the heaviness of the intruder's anger and I had a very strong urge to run away from it. I couldn't pinpoint who the anger was being directed at."

"It's too bad the women share an office," Jenna said. "It would be easier to figure out who the intended victim is if only one person used that office."

"Having three people sharing an office room is definitely working to the intruder's advantage," Mr. Finch said.

"I'm worried about when the intruder will strike again." Angie poured the batter into a cake pan. "If he wants to get at someone in particular, he might end up striking when other people are around. That means more possible victims."

"Or," Jenna's eyes widened. "He might strike when the victim is at home in order to avoid the office filled with people."

Angie's stomach sank. "Monica, Bev, and Lydia need to be on guard. There's no telling when or where the person will strike. The women need to be ready."

Angie, Chief Martin, and Mr. Finch sat in Monica and Ted Windsor's living room. The couple told the chief that they wanted to help any way they could to catch the intruder.

"I'm worried he'll become bold and will attack

one of us." Monica looked to the room's entryway to be sure her children weren't listening at the door.

Ted took her hand. "If this guy dares come to our home, he'll have both of us to deal with."

Chief Martin asked if Monica or Ted had a run-in with anyone recently.

"No one." Ted looked to his wife for agreement. "We haven't been involved in anything at all."

"We get along with our co-workers, we like our jobs, we get along with our neighbors and friends," Monica said. "That is, when we have the time to see them. Our lives are consumed with our jobs and the two kids. We don't have much free time at all … which limits our chances of running into some nut who might decide to hurt one of us because he claims we looked at him sideways or something."

Ted chuckled. "There are some advantages to staying home in the evening."

Mr. Finch asked, "You don't recall an argument or disagreement with someone at work?"

Both of the young parents shook their heads.

"A disagreement with *anyone* recently?"

"No, nothing at all," Monica said, and Ted agreed.

"What about Lydia?" Angie asked. "She's

recently divorced. Do you know if she's had trouble with anyone?"

Monica took a quick look at her husband, and then turned back to Angie. "Lydia's husband is a pain. He's always trying to get in touch with her. He doesn't seem very smart about relationships or about how people are feeling. Roger was seeing another woman and Monica found out about it. She told him she didn't care to see him ever again. The fling didn't work out, the younger woman left Roger, and he's been trying to crawl back ever since. Lydia won't get back together with him. Never in a millions years. She's not really having trouble with anyone. Roger is just a pest. He's a baby. He wanted something else, it didn't work out, and he hurried back to what he had first hoping he could go back to the way things used to be."

"What about Bev?" Finch questioned. "Has she had some trouble with anyone?"

Again, Monica shook her head. "Bev's a sweetheart. No one would ever hurt her. Everyone likes Bev. She's always so helpful whenever we get things messed up on our laptops or desktops." Monica sighed. "I'm a smart woman. I can fix things. I can work fulltime and run a home, but I don't know what on earth to do when something stops working on my laptop. Bev always helps, and she does it with a smile. I can't imagine what she could do to set someone against her."

"Bev broke up with her boyfriend recently," the chief said.

"They weren't really boyfriend-girlfriend," Monica pointed out. "They dated, maybe once a week, if that. It was only for a few months. They agreed they weren't the right match so they moved on. It wasn't a big deal."

"You know," Ted said, "I just remembered something."

All eyes turned to the man.

"Monica and I were planning to go out to dinner after work about three weeks ago. Her mom was watching the kids for us. After I got out of work, I walked over to Brighter Days to meet her. I texted when I got there and waited outside for her to come out. I had some good news to share that day. I'd been given a substantial raise and a nice bonus. When she came out, I hugged her and told her the news." Ted looked to his wife. "You reached up and kissed me."

"I remember." Monica smiled.

Ted went on. "When we turned to go to the restaurant, I noticed a guy watching us. He looked really angry. As we passed him, he swore at us, called us dirty names, made a rude gesture."

Monica nodded. "We hurried away. I was afraid he would follow us, but he didn't. He just stood on the sidewalk staring at the Brighter Days building." The woman shuddered at the thought of the incident. "I'd forgotten about it. At the time, it made me feel uneasy, a little nervous."

"Do you remember what he looked like?" Chief Martin asked.

Ted and Monica looked at each other.

"He had on a big heavy jacket," Monica said.

"The hood was up," Ted recalled. "I don't really remember what his face looked like. It was hard to see with the hood around the face. I don't think I'd recognize him if I saw him again."

"I don't think I would either," Monica agreed. "He just stood there so I didn't get a chance to see how he walked. I can't even venture a guess about how old he was. He had on a knitted hat, pulled down to the tops of his eyes, and the hood was up. It was hard to get a sense of what he looked like."

"I do remember feeling that flight or fight reaction," Ted said. "My adrenaline was flowing. I was ready to pop him one if he became more aggressive.

I was glad he stayed where he was and didn't threaten us."

"Had you noticed the man anytime previously?" the chief asked Monica.

"No, I'd never seen him before. At least, not that I recalled. I often park out back and leave through the rear door. Maybe he's been out front before, but I'd never encountered him."

"Did you talk to Lydia or Bev about the man? Did you bring him up the next day at work?" Angie asked.

"The next morning, I didn't remember the guy bothered us the night before. The interaction was very brief, a few seconds." Monica shook her head. "He completely slipped out of my head. I'd better bring it up with Lydia and Bev. Maybe one of them has seen the guy on another occasion. Maybe he just likes to hassle people as they walk by. He's probably harmless."

Angie felt a shiver run through her veins.

8

Bev Tarant's former boyfriend, Allen Poulin, was thirty-two-years old, stood about five feet nine inches tall, was lean, and had brown eyes and dark brown hair that was cut a little longer in a shaggy, mussed style probably due to the natural wave in the hair. The man was professionally dressed in dark slacks and an off-white buttoned-down shirt. It was late in the afternoon when Angie, Courtney, and Chief Martin met Allen at a coffee shop across from the office building where he worked.

"I'm an electrical engineer at Nautilus Engineering." Allen waved his hand at the window indicating the brick building in the office park on the other side of the highway. "I've been there for four years."

"How did you meet Bev?" Chief Martin asked.

"Through an associate of mine. He and I had gone out for a drink after work. He knew a woman who was at the bar. Bev was the woman's friend. We talked, hit it off. She's a smart person, easy to talk to."

"You dated for a while?" Angie asked.

"Just a few months. We decided to move on." Allen pushed at his curly bangs.

"Why did you make that decision?" Courtney kept her blue eyes on Allen's face.

Allen shrugged and lifted his coffee mug. "We're both busy, we both have things we enjoy doing after work. We live almost forty minutes from each other. It was hard to make the time for one another."

"What hobbies do you enjoy?" Angie asked.

Allen's gaze seemed intense giving the impression he was annoyed by the question. "I hike, even in the winter. I do a lot of skiing. Bev doesn't have any interest in those things. They're important to me. I like to get outdoors after working inside all day. I knew we weren't right for each other when I discovered she had no interest in the two activities I enjoy the most."

"Did you initiate the end of the relationship?" the chief questioned.

"I don't think you could label it a relationship. We dated briefly and not often. The last time we went out we talked about not seeing each other anymore ... that things weren't really working between us. Bev's great, but we weren't right for each other. It was no big deal."

"Did you know that the non-profit where Bev works was broken into recently?" the chief asked.

"I saw it in the news. No one was hurt, right? Someone broke in after work hours?" Allen took a swallow of his coffee.

"That's right. Someone broke in twice. There was some damage done."

Allen lifted an eyebrow. "There are security cameras in there. Did they help you determine who the person is?"

Chief Martin straightened. As with Lydia's ex-husband, he didn't intend to share important details of the case with Allen. "They weren't that helpful. Had you been in the offices?"

Allen cleared his throat. "I met Bev there a couple of times. She was working late so I met her at the office so we could walk to a restaurant from there. I went inside briefly."

"You noticed the security cameras?" the chief asked.

"Sure. I'm an engineer. I work with sensitive

technological information at Nautilus. I notice the things around me."

The little blond hairs on Angie's arms stood up. Allen seemed a little cocky and arrogant, not so much in the things he said, but in the way he said them.

"What did you think of the office setup?" Courtney questioned.

"There isn't enough space. People are on top of each other. Bev shared a very small office with two or three other workers. It was like a cave. I couldn't function in there. I need space and quiet in order to think, not people buzzing in and out or talking on the phones." Allen shook his head at the thought of it.

Courtney said, "I meant what did you think of the security setup, not the office configuration."

Allen looked taken aback that he'd misinterpreted the question. "Oh. It was adequate from what I saw. Rudimentary, at best, but I don't think they need anything more than what they have there ... the cameras, the door locks. There isn't anything important or classified in those offices."

Angie thought Brighter Days would probably disagree with Allen that the office files didn't contain anything very important.

"Are you seeing anyone at the moment?" Chief Martin asked.

Allen's brow furrowed. "I'm not. Why is that relevant?"

The chief smiled reassuringly. "It's simply gathering information about the people around the workers at Brighter Days."

"I'm not around any of the workers," Allen said seriously.

"But you were," Chief Martin nodded. "It's important to speak with everyone connected to the non-profit, however remotely. You were present in the office a couple of times. You might have seen something that could help the case."

Allen said, "I didn't see anything. There's nothing I can tell you that would be helpful."

The chief shrugged a shoulder. "You'd be surprised at how many times I've heard that from someone who turned out to know a vital detail."

"Not in this case, I'm afraid," Allen said. "There wasn't anyone else in the offices when I was there with Bev. I was inside for ten minutes at most. I wish I could share something that would help, but I didn't see anything at all. Just a crowded office space shared by multiple people that isn't big enough for one person alone. I don't know how they get away with stuffing workers in like that. Isn't there a fire code or something?"

Chief Martin ignored the question. "When was the last time you saw Bev?"

"Um. Let's see. Three weeks ago, maybe."

"So it hasn't been long since you both decided not to pursue a relationship," Angie observed.

"Right. Three or four weeks. I can't remember exactly. I could go through my texts if you need to know."

Angie asked, "Did Bev ever mention that she might be worried for her safety?"

Allen's eyes widened. "No. Never. Why would she be?"

Angie asked a follow-up. "Did Bev mention that one of her colleagues might be worried about his or her personal safety?"

Allen scoffed. "No. They don't work at a nuclear plant or at a detective agency or for the FBI. They work at a non-profit. Who cares about that?"

Angie didn't like the man's dismissive attitude.

Courtney said, "Some of the clients they work with at Brighter Days might be difficult."

"I don't see why they would be. People get help at that place."

Courtney decided to drop the topic. "Have you lived on the North Shore for a long time?"

"Four years. Before that I lived in Boston. Too many people, too much traffic there. I like being out of the city and closer to nature."

"Did you grow up in the city?" Angie asked.

Allen shook his head. "I grew up in western Massachusetts."

"Where did you go to college?"

"The University of Massachusetts in Amherst." Allen shifted in his seat. "Why?"

"No particular reason," Angie said. "My sisters and I lived in Boston for a long time. We enjoyed the city, but we prefer the small town feel of Sweet Cove."

"When you dated Bev," the chief asked, "did she talk about her co-workers much? Did any of them have something going on in their personal lives that was bothersome?"

Allen started to shake his head, but he stopped and looked at the chief. "Bev's friend, the director of the place, Lydia something or other, was recently divorced. Bev said the ex-husband was a pain. He kept badgering Lydia, asking her to meet, asking her to reconsider the break-up of the marriage. He sounded like he was desperate or something. Who knows why? There are plenty of women out there. Move on."

Angie asked, "Did Bev say anything about Lydia being uneasy about her ex-husband's contact with her?"

"Bev said Lydia thought the guy was a pain. She didn't say anything about Lydia being afraid of him," Allen told them. "I guess she did mention once that Lydia said she should get a bodyguard, but I thought Bev was kidding. Maybe she wasn't." Allen remembered something. "The other woman Bev shared the office with ... Monica. I heard her say something about hoping that Lydia's ex-husband wouldn't be hanging around in the parking lot."

"When did you see Monica?" Chief Martin asked.

"When I went inside to meet Bev one time."

"Was that after-hours?"

"Yeah, it was."

"I thought Bev was alone in the office the two times you went inside to meet her?"

"Yeah, well, Monica was there one time when I went in. She left before we did. I only saw her for a minute. I forgot she was there."

Angie wondered what else Allen might have forgotten about.

"What did she mean about Lydia's ex-husband being in the parking lot?" Courtney asked.

"Bev told me that sometimes the guy would park in the lot behind Brighter Days waiting for Lydia to come out."

"Why did he do that?"

Allen made a face. "To be a pain would be my guess."

"Did the ex-husband harass Lydia?"

"I didn't ask. Nobody seemed concerned about it."

"Did Bev say any more about the ex-husband being out in the lot?"

"No. She didn't bring it up when we were out. The guy sounded neurotic though. He was supposed to be an important lawyer. I don't know how he could be some big attorney. He sounded weak to me. Lydia didn't want anything more to do with him. Why doesn't he just leave her alone?" Allen smiled. "Maybe Lydia is independently wealthy. Maybe she inherited a bunch of money and the ex-husband doesn't like losing access to the fortune." He chuckled. "I guess the guy should have thought about the money before he went running around."

Angie stared at Allen and thought Bev probably made the right decision to stop seeing him.

9

Angie had showered and was wearing a fluffy robe and slippers when she walked down the hallway to Jenna's jewelry studio. Euclid and Circe were sitting on the sofa by the window, their eyes glued onto Jenna and Orla who were sitting at the round table by a golden fire blazing in the fireplace, but when Angie came in, the cats jumped down to greet her. Petting the felines, Angie looked over to the women.

"It sure is cozy in here."

When Angie took a seat at the table with her sister and Orla, she noticed the serious expressions on their faces.

"What's wrong? Has something happened? Are you okay?"

Jenna gave her twin sister a smile. "I'm fine. Orla and I have been talking about Mom."

A shot of adrenaline rushed through Angie as she looked from Jenna to Orla. "What about her?" she asked tentatively.

"Jenna told me again that you and she have been thinking about the circumstances surrounding your mother's death." Orla folded her hands on the table.

Angie nodded and said with a soft voice, "With the babies coming, we've been thinking a lot about her."

"It's understandable to miss someone when important things happen." Orla put her hand over Angie's for a moment. "Your mother was taken too soon."

Sadness tugged at Angie's heart and her eyes misted over before she cleared her throat. "What have you been talking about?"

Jenna pushed at her bangs. "Orla knows some people."

Angie looked at the older woman. "People?"

"The community has had questions about your mother's *accident*," Orla said.

"Which community would that be?" Angie asked in a shaky voice.

"The community that you and your sisters are a part of."

Angie didn't know what to ask.

"There are people in every town and city who have special skills like you and your sisters do," Orla explained. "I think you've sensed that this is the case."

Angie and Jenna shared a look.

"We help each other, we protect each other, we look out for one another," Orla said. "Your grandmother and your mother were part of this community."

"Mom?" Angie asked. "We've talked about whether or not Mom had skills. If she did, we think she didn't accept them."

"Your mother had very powerful abilities, but she was reluctant to develop them. In a way, they frightened her."

"Just like Ellie," Jenna pointed out. "Ellie would be happy if our skills would disappear and never come back."

Orla smiled. "Ellie and Elizabeth are very similar in personality and temperament."

"And Ellie looks the most like Mom, too," Angie said.

"I don't know much about your mother's accident. The community doesn't either, but some think what happened to Elizabeth was deliberate."

Jenna let out a little gasp.

"Someone killed her?" Angie placed her hand over her abdomen as if to shield her unborn daughter from danger. "Why? Why would someone hurt our mother?"

A voice from the room's entrance said, "Perhaps that is something we can find out together." Mr. Finch leaned on his cane as he entered the jewelry studio and joined the women at the table. Circe jumped up on the man's lap and he stroked her ebony fur while Euclid leapt onto the empty chair beside him.

"Mr. Finch and I have been discussing the accident," Orla said moving her eyes from Jenna to Angie.

"We know you both have been thinking about what happened to your mother," Finch said.

"Your powers will be growing stronger with the birth of your children," Orla told the sisters. "If the two of you and Ellie and Courtney would like to look into the cause of Elizabeth's death, then Mr. Finch and I will help you."

Ellie and Courtney came into the room carrying

trays with sweets, a teapot, and teacups, and stood near the threshold.

"We heard what you said," Courtney told them. "I'm in."

"Is it dangerous?" Ellie asked in a small voice.

Orla answered with a serious expression. "Yes."

Ellie nodded, pushed her shoulders back, and took a deep breath. "I'm in, too."

Euclid trilled his approval.

"What do you think, sis?" Jenna asked her twin.

"When do we start?" Angie said with conviction.

Finch smiled at the sisters. "Not before the babies are born."

Ellie and Courtney set the trays of refreshments in the middle of the round table and Orla lifted the silver pot and poured the tea into the cups.

"About six months after the babies arrive, your powers will have increased," Orla explained. "We'll wait until then to start our investigation."

"Okay." Angie placed a chocolate chip cookie on her plate. "That will be next July then."

Courtney glanced at the crackling fire and then turned to her family and friends. "Whoever is responsible for our mother's death better get ready ... because we're coming for you." She raised her teacup, and the others lifted theirs and clinked them together while the two cats threw back their heads and howled.

An hour later, Angie and Josh and Jenna and Tom were sitting on the sofas near the fire discussing the latest family news. Euclid was pressed up against Josh's leg, sound asleep, and Circe was perched on Tom's lap with her eyes closed.

With his arm around his wife, Josh said, "I can't say I'm crazy about the idea of you and Jenna heading to Boston to hunt down your mother's killer, but I know it has to be done. I understand that your powers come with responsibility."

"It's like being married to secret agents." Tom held Jenna's hand in his. "Can you two retire from your duties and give up on the paranormal stuff?" He shook his head with a wistful smile. "Don't bother answering. I know you can't do that."

"Tom and I don't have any special powers, but we'll do whatever we can to help you," Josh told them.

Angie snuggled close and rested her head against her husband's chest. "You two are the best."

Josh placed his hand on Angie's abdomen. "I can feel Gigi kicking."

"These babies are going to add a whole new, wonderful dimension to our lives," Tom said with pride. "I can't wait to meet them."

"And I can't believe they're due in three weeks." Jenna squeezed Tom's hand. "Is everyone ready for sleepless nights?"

The four of them groaned.

"What about the current case?" Josh asked. "Is there any chance of solving it before the babies come?"

"I don't know." Angie let out a sigh. "Mr. Finch and I talked about it this afternoon in the bake shop. We both feel that someone is in serious danger. None of us feel that the break-ins at Brighter Days are only break-ins. The second time the intruder entered the non-profit, he was violent ... he damaged and smashed things ... he made a threat by leaving a bullet and handcuffs on one of the desks."

"Things are escalating," Jenna said. "And it isn't going to end with the threat."

"You think the intruder is aiming to hurt some-one?" Josh asked. "Someone in particular?"

"Yes," Angie said. "I just don't know who the target is."

"We need to figure out the target," Jenna told them. "If we know who the target is, it might be easier to determine who the intruder is."

"The trespasser left the bullet on Bev's desk," Tom said. "Is the intended victim Bev Tarant or was leaving it on her desk a decoy?"

"I don't know." Angie rubbed at her temple.

Jenna said, "We're going to ask Chief Martin if Mr. Finch can hold the bullet in his hand to see if he can pick up something about the intruder."

"Good idea," Josh said. "Is it possible that the victim is someone other than Bev, Lydia, or Monica?"

"It's possible," Angie said. "But I don't think it's likely."

"We all think it has to be one of the three women who share that office," Jenna said. "Why else would the intruder linger near their room?"

"The criminal must know there are security cameras in the offices," Tom said. "He or she must know the cameras are capturing his or her movements. So is he putting on a performance to throw off law enforcement? Is he keeping his intentions secret? Or does he not care that officers are observing what he's doing?"

"He could be thumbing his nose at law enforcement," Josh said. "He might think he's invincible. He might have the idea that no one will be able to figure out what he's up to."

"I get a bad feeling from this case," Angie said. "I think the intruder is going to make his move soon. We don't have a lot of time."

"What will you and Chief Martin do next?" Josh asked.

"We're going to interview the three officemates again," Angie said. "Monica and her husband reported that a man swore at them outside the Brighter Days offices. Chief Martin is looking to see if any businesses near Brighter Days have outside security cameras that might have caught the guy on tape."

"Officers are speaking with people at businesses in the area to see if anyone has seen this man before or if anyone has had an interaction with him," Jenna said. "They're hoping to get a description of him."

"We need to come up with answers," Angie said.

"You will," Josh told his wife. "There hasn't been a case yet that all of you haven't solved."

"It has to be soon. We don't have any time to waste. We have to figure this out." Angie's eyes showed the extent of her worry. "Or I'm afraid someone is going to die."

10

The former employee of Brighter Days, Joelle Young, lived in an apartment just one town away from Silver Cove and Sweet Cove. She wore no makeup and her blond hair was cut very short. She had on a tight red shirt that didn't do anything to hide the woman's muscular shoulders and arms. Joelle gave Angie the impression that she could snap you in half if she had a mind to do so.

The apartment was spacious and nicely decorated with modern furniture in muted tones. There was no clutter and nothing looked out of place.

Chief Martin and Angie took seats in the living room.

"I heard about the break-ins at the non-profit."

Joelle sat ramrod straight. "You must have heard that I got fired from there."

"We've spoken with people at Brighter Days," the chief nodded.

"You suspect me for the break-ins, I suppose."

"We're interviewing people who work at or have recently worked at the non-profit trying to gather information," Chief Martin said.

"I don't know anything about it." Joelle had a pout on her face.

"Was there anyone there who made trouble?"

"You mean besides me?"

"Would you like to tell us what happened with you at Brighter Days?" Angie asked in a gentle voice.

"Not really." Joelle crossed her arms over her chest in a defensive posture. "What exactly have you heard?"

"A colleague suggested that you might have taken something from her purse?" Angie said.

Joelle laughed. "Might have? You're very diplomatic. I doubt Bev Tarant was diplomatic about it."

"What happened?" It was pretty clear that Joelle wanted to talk about the incident and Angie wished the woman would just say what she had to say.

"I took some money from Bev's wallet. I also took two credit cards out of the wallet. I was planning to put it all back. I was stuck for money and payday wasn't for a week. I hoped to borrow some of Bev's money until I got paid. It was wrong, plain and simple. I was feeling desperate and did something stupid."

"Did you try to explain to Bev what you did?" Angie questioned.

Joelle took in a long breath as her face hardened. "No, I did not. Bev doesn't like me. It wouldn't have helped for me to say anything. I got caught red-handed. She wouldn't have listened to me. I did something wrong and paid the price. I take responsibility for it."

"How did you like working at the non-profit?"

"It was a job. I had to share an office with three other people. I prefer to work alone. Having people around is jarring to me. I didn't have any privacy. When I accepted the job, I didn't know I'd be shoved into a room with other people. I'm afraid my job performance suffered because I felt stressed."

"Did you like some of your co-workers?"

"I didn't like the women in my office. They were always yakking about their problems, an-ex-husband, a guy one of them was dating, the other woman's kids. It was very boring to me and I didn't have anything to contribute so I didn't speak."

"Where you looking for another job?"

"I was actually, but I didn't find anything before I got fired."

"Have you found something new?" Angie asked.

"Not yet. I don't want to make the same mistake and end up in a situation that isn't right for me. I'm taking my time."

Angie nodded. "Did you grow up around here?"

"I grew up in Seattle, Washington. I went to school at the University of Pennsylvania. I got a degree in math and then decided to join the Army."

"Where did you serve?" Chief Martin asked although he'd heard Joelle had been overseas.

Joelle told them where she'd served and when. "I don't like to talk about it so please don't ask any more questions about my service."

Angie and the chief respected the request.

"Do you have family back in Washington?"

"My parents and a sister."

"Are you close with one another?"

"I wouldn't say so. We see each other at holidays. We're pleasant to one another, but we don't have much in common."

"What do your parents do?"

"They're both schoolteachers, my sister is a teacher, too."

"You look like you work out a lot," Angie noted.

"I enjoy being strong and fit," Joelle said.

"What's your workout schedule like?"

"I work out every day. Weights, running, tai chi. I bike, swim, and row when the weather is better. I do some athletic competitions. I usually do well."

"What gym do you go to?"

Joelle told her the name of the place. "There are weights and machines in the basement workout room here in the apartment building, too. It was convenient when I was working."

"How do you spend your day?"

"I work out twice a day. I do errands. I look for a job. I watch movies and read. The day goes by fast."

"Was there anyone at the non-profit you thought might be a troublemaker?" the chief asked. "An employee? A client?"

Joelle shook her head. "I didn't get to know anyone well and I didn't come in contact with the clients, only in passing. I don't know anyone there you could describe as a troublemaker. That doesn't mean there isn't someone there who might be trouble. I just didn't come across them."

"How did you end up in this area of Massachusetts?"

"I like the ocean. I didn't want to go back to

Washington. It rains too much there for me. Someone I knew in the Army had visited Sweet Cove and told me how much he liked it. I searched for a job in the area thinking it was as good a place to try as any. I got the job and moved here."

"Have you met some people you like?"

Joelle shrugged. "The people at the gym. They're no-nonsense. I like that. Not always blabbing about their personal lives. Anyway, I don't mind being alone. Most people are really into socializing. Not me. I prefer being alone most of the time."

"Are you dating?"

"No, I'm not."

"Was there anyone at work who seemed to hold a grudge against someone?"

"Bev Tarant, but I guess I can't blame her."

"Anyone else?"

"I really don't know. I worked in my shared office. I didn't talk to the other employees much."

"Did you ever witness an argument or a fight between any of the people there?"

"I didn't."

"Did you ever notice anyone unusual hanging around outside?"

"No. Just normal people walking around or

waiting for a bus. There are a lot of offices and businesses in the area, a lot of people coming and going."

"Did any of your office-mates mention being afraid or worried about someone?"

Joelle said, "Lydia always complained about her ex-husband, but her tone was disgusted. She isn't afraid of him."

"Nobody mentioned a run-in with anyone inside or outside of work?" the chief asked.

"I don't remember anything like that."

"What about Monica? Was she having any trouble with a babysitter? Did she get into a fender bender with anyone? Did she have an argument at a store with anyone?"

Joelle rolled her eyes. "Monica talked about her husband and kids all the time. She talked about everything that was going on with them. She talked about everything that was going on with her. If she had an issue with anyone, she wouldn't have held back. She would have talked about it until I needed to block my ears. So no, she didn't mention any trouble with anyone while I was in the room."

"I understand that you don't want to talk about your time in the military," the chief said.

Joelle's eyes darkened as she looked at the man across from her.

"But I have one question. Would you mind telling us if you received an honorable discharge?"

Joelle's lips tightened into a thin line. "Yes ... I did." She checked her watch. "I'm going to the gym in a few minutes. Are we done here? I'd like to get ready to go."

The look the woman gave Chief Martin caused Angie to shiver.

"Yes, we can be done," the chief said. "We appreciate your help. Thanks for taking the time to speak with us."

Angie had been having a hard time reading Joelle. The woman was clearly dedicated to her fitness routine, she seemed to know herself well and realized she couldn't work in close proximity to others, she was a loner and seemed content with that part of her personality. She must be disciplined from being in the Army. Then why did she make such a mistake as stealing from a co-worker? Why did she think she would get away with taking cash and credit cards from Bev Tarant? It seemed like an out-of-character action. What could have nudged her to do that? Angie decided to ask some quick questions about Joelle's financial state before they left the apartment.

She stayed seated on the sofa and asked, "Are you able to collect unemployment benefits?"

Joelle shook her head. "I can't. I wasn't laid off. I was fired."

"You weren't in the military long enough to get a pension, were you?"

"Definitely not."

"Do you have savings to tide you over until you find a job?"

"Some. I really need to get going." Joelle stood up, ending the meeting.

11

———

In one of the meeting rooms at Brighter Days, Lydia Hendricks sat across from Police Chief Martin and Angie at a scuffed, old wooden table.

"Have you been in touch with your ex-husband recently?" the chief asked.

"He texts. I don't usually answer. Should I classify that as *being in touch*?"

"Do you respond to the texts?" Angie questioned.

"If I do, it's to tell him I don't have time to chat." Lydia shook her head.

"You still have the impression that Roger wants to get back together?"

Lydia chuckled. "Yes, I do."

"Do you have a security system at your home?" Chief Martin asked.

"We have one, but it doesn't work. It's been years since I thought about having it fixed. Why bother? Roger isn't going to break in," Lydia said. "I changed all the locks on the doors and windows. I didn't want him using his key to make an unexpected appearance."

"Have you started dating?" Angie asked, and the question almost made Lydia spit out the mouthful of water she had taken in.

"I wasn't expecting that question. I went out to dinner with a nice man about three weeks ago," Lydia said. "I found a dating website for middle-aged people online. I thought what the heck. Even though the man was pleasant, I didn't want to see him again."

"Why not?" Angie asked with a kind tone.

Lydia leaned back in her chair with a sigh. "It seemed so weird and foreign. I'm not ready to date. I felt very awkward."

"The date was prior to the break-ins?" Angie questioned.

"It was." Lydia's eyes widened. "Oh, no. The man I dated isn't the one who broke in here. He wasn't the type to do that. His manner was gentle and kind. We discussed how hard it was to start dating again. He was very understanding about my feelings." Lydia said, "You know, thinking about it, I really enjoyed being out with the man. Maybe I should initiate contact with him and try to get over feeling so strange about seeing someone new."

"Does Roger know you went out on a date?" Chief Martin asked.

"He knows." Lydia's face tensed and she rolled her eyes. "I don't know how he found out, but he texted me the following day and asked if I had fun with the new man. I didn't respond to him."

"Did you share with a friend that you were going out on a date?" Chief Martin asked.

"I told a few friends. I told my sister."

"One of them must have spoken to Roger."

"I don't know who would have done that," Lydia said.

Angie asked, "I don't like to ask this, but have you ever caught Roger following you?"

Lydia's face hardened. "When we first divorced, I saw Roger tailing me. I was furious. I got out of my car and yelled at him. It happened three times. The last time, I threatened to call the police and report him, and I haven't caught him doing it again."

"But it's possible he *is* doing it," Chief Martin warned the woman.

"He'd better not be."

The chief said, "We've heard that Roger sometimes lingers in the parking lot behind the building to speak with you when you come out."

Lydia sighed. "He did that a few times until I had a fit and screamed at him. He hasn't been back."

"How long ago did you see Roger in the lot?"

"Oh, let's see." Lydia tapped a pen on the tabletop while she thought. "I don't remember exactly. Two weeks ago?"

"Does Roger continue to text you?" Angie asked.

"Yes, he does. Sometimes a few days go by without any communication from him, then I get a flurry of texts. He asks how I am, how the boys are, would I like to meet for dinner. It's always the same. If I reply, I tell him I'm fine, I'm busy, and I can't talk."

"Did you meet Allen Poulin? The man Bev was dating?" Chief Martin questioned.

"I met him once in passing. He picked Bev up in the parking lot. She and I were leaving the office together and she introduced me to him as we passed his car."

"Did you get any impressions about him?"

"Allen was dressed professionally. He shook my hand. We exchanged a few words. That was it," Lydia explained. "That was the only time I saw him."

The interview came to a close and Lydia went to ask Monica Windsor to come to speak with Angie and Chief Martin.

Monica was her usual warm, cheerful self. "How are things going? Did you find the nut yet?"

"We're still investigating," Chief Martin informed the woman. "Have you run into the man who bothered you and your husband out in front of the building the other evening?"

"I haven't, but I go out the back door every night to get my car from the lot. No one has mentioned someone lingering outside," Monica said. "It must have been someone who was passing by that night and not someone who hangs around this part of town."

"Have you had any other unusual interactions with anyone?" Angie asked.

"No." Monica's brown hair shined under the overhead lights. "Everything is the same as it always is." The young woman hesitated for a few moments. "There *was* something. I worked late the other night and I was the last one to leave. I headed out to my car, and for a quick second, I thought I saw someone watching me."

"Where was the person standing?"

"It was probably only my imagination." Monica

forced a smile. "Or maybe the shadows under the lights."

"Where did you think you saw the person?" Angie asked again.

"At the corner of the lot near the street. There are trees at the edge of the parking lot. I thought someone was standing under the trees, but when I looked again, there wasn't anyone there." Monica's shoulders hunched together. "I think the intruder has me spooked. It's always dark when I leave the building and if I'm the only one heading out, I get a little nervous and worried. I'm afraid I'll run into the trespasser so I always rush out and hurry to my car and slam the door shut. I know it's silly to be so anxious."

"It's completely normal to have those worries," Angie told her. "It's self-preservation. You're trying to protect yourself."

"I know." Monica nodded. "But the intruder isn't going to be hanging around in the lot waiting for everyone to clear out of the building. I'm over-reacting."

"When you thought you saw someone near the trees, did you notice anything about him? What he looked like? What he was wearing?" Angie questioned.

"I didn't. It was so quick. And anyway, I most likely imagined seeing the person." Monica looked at Chief Martin. "It will be such a relief when you catch the guy."

The chief gave a reassuring nod and then asked, "Do you remember meeting Bev's date, Allen Poulin?"

"Sure. I remember. I met him in the office one evening when he came by to pick up Bev. He was good-looking. Seemed athletic. He's an electrical engineer so he must be smart. He was dressed nicely." Monica shrugged a shoulder. "He wasn't all that friendly, but I guess he didn't want to hang around an office talking with Bev's coworkers. I'm sure he wanted to go to the restaurant with Bev."

"What gave you the impression he wasn't being friendly?" Angie asked.

Monica tilted her head in thought. "It's hard to pinpoint the reason. Allen didn't make eye contact for long. He answered my questions and then looked to Bev. I realize now that he didn't ask me anything at all. He seemed disinterested, slightly bored. I think he wanted to get going."

"Would you call him rude?"

"Not rude, really. Kind of abrupt ... sort of detached."

"How did he and Bev interact?" Angie questioned.

"Like you'd expect from people who are getting to know each other. A little stiff with one another," Monica said. "But I didn't get the impression they were that into each other. You know how some people are when they're with someone new? Sort of giddy, happy, smiling at each other all the time, making eye contact, touching. That thrill of newness and attraction. I didn't see that with them."

"Did you ask Bev how they were getting along?" Angie questioned.

"Yeah, I did. She said Allen was nice, but kind of standoffish. He didn't hold her hand when they were out, things like that were missing. Bev wondered if Allen needed time to warm up. I bet he never did warm up and that's one of the reasons she stopped seeing him."

"Has Bev dated since she stopped seeing Allen?"

Monica smiled. "Not yet, but she met someone the other night when she was at a party with some friends. She thinks they'll go out. She seems excited about it. I hope she and the new guy click. I know Bev would love to have a husband and a couple of kids one day." Monica laughed. "She still wants those things even after seeing me pull my hair out somedays. Bev knows I wouldn't trade my life for anything." Glancing at Angie's round belly, Monica asked, "Is it your first?"

Angie nodded. "She's due soon."

"Congratulations." Monica's voice was full of tenderness. "The best part of your life is about to begin."

12

"This is Dr. Reilly Henderson." Chief Martin introduced Angie, Jenna, and Mr. Finch to the psychologist who had been consulting with the police on the Brighter Days case.

Around thirty-years old, Dr. Henderson was petite and slim with intense blue eyes and long brown hair. She had a calm and friendly manner.

"Dr. Henderson is working with us to provide some characteristics we should look for as we try to find the person responsible for the break-ins. I've asked her to give us a summary of the profile she worked up on the Brighter Days intruder."

Everyone took seats around the old conference table.

With a pleasant smile, the psychologist said to

the two Roseland sisters and Mr. Finch, "Please call me Reilly. Chief Martin tells me you've been invaluable to him on many cases. I'm very happy to meet you."

Angie wondered what Chief Martin told Reilly about them.

Reilly said, "I understand you've all seen the security tapes taken from the non-profit. To recap … in the first tapes, we see the intruder walking calmly through the offices. He is not in a hurry. He is not rushed. I refer to the person as a *he* because it's convenient. We don't know if the person is male or female. When the intruder paid his first visit to the offices, he did not damage anything. He simply spent his time observing."

"Do you think his intention was to get a feel for the place or was he waiting and hoping to run into someone?" Jenna asked.

"I wondered the same thing," Reilly said. "But after watching the tapes many times over, I think he was there to look around. I don't think he wanted to run into anyone. I think it was a calculated part of his plan to carefully memorize the layout of the place with the intention of returning."

"Which he did," Finch said.

Reilly nodded. "His second visit was quite

different from the first. While inside the offices on the second visit, he deliberately moved through the halls and rooms. If a room was locked, he smashed it open with the baseball bat. If the room was unlocked, he went inside and damaged a single item that was located in the room. Every time and without fail, when he entered an unlocked room, he destroyed one thing, and only one thing."

"It's odd behavior, isn't it?" Angie asked.

"It seems odd, but it's actually a planned and controlled action. This person is able to manage his anger. He makes a plan and he does not deviate from it."

"What do you make of his only entering the rooms that were unlocked?" Finch asked the psychologist. "In my mind, I would expect him to enter the rooms that were locked. I would expect him to damage an item in a room that had been locked as a punishment for trying to keep him out."

"Very clever thinking, Mr. Finch," Reilly told the man. "But I think this intruder is reserving punishment for those who *didn't* lock their doors. He's sending a message to them. Lock your door. Protect yourselves. Take precautions. Because if you don't, your belongings will be damaged or lost, your space will be invaded."

Finch nodded. "I see."

"For those who *did* lock their rooms," Reilly went on, "the message was this: it doesn't matter if you lock your doors. If I want to get in, I will. If I want to hurt you, I will. You are powerless before me."

Angie felt her stomach roil.

"This person believes he can do anything," Reilly said. "He believes he can't be stopped. He has some fantasy of his moral superiority."

"The intruder left two items on a desk in one of the offices," Jenna said. "Obviously, that was another message."

"A bullet and a pair of handcuffs," Reilly said with a nod. "The message from the intruder can be interpreted as him telling others that if he wants to kill, he will do it. If he wants to subdue you, he will do that. The man is a true believer in his own power."

"Have you come up with a profile for who might be doing this?" Angie asked.

"The profile can change according to new information that is gathered," Reilly said. "Right now, we have a good idea of who we're dealing with. The intruder is a male who is probably in his late-twenties to early-fifties. He might have a professional job. He is most likely intelligent, cunning. He may or may not see that his own actions have consequences ... it might depend on the circumstances. He is rule-based. He lacks empathy. He believes wrong-doers should be punished. What constitutes wrong-doing is up to him, of course. He is the lawmaker, the judge, and the jury."

Angie swallowed to clear the tightness in her throat. "Do you think the intruder will act on his threat of violence symbolized by the bullet he left behind?"

"Yes." Reilly's face was somber. "And I believe he will act quickly."

"Do you think he left the bullet on the desk of the person he's targeting?" Jenna questioned.

"That's hard to answer. He may have left the things on the desk as a broad threat. He probably doesn't plan to reveal the specific someone he has an issue with. He may have a target in mind, but he may not be willing to publically indicate who it is," Reilly said. "So no, the person whose desk has the bullet on it is not necessarily the intruder's target, and it could be dangerous to focus on the safety of only the person who sits at that desk. The intended victim could be anyone who works at Brighter Days."

"Okay," Jenna said. "Then I need to keep a broader view of who the intended victim might be.

Do you think the intruder knows his victim well or could the intruder be someone with a very superficial connection to the victim?"

"I don't think it's a superficial connection," Reilly said. "I think there's been a good amount of interaction between the intruder and the intended victim. The intruder has probably been inside the Brighter Days offices before he broke in. From watching the tapes, I believe he knows the positions and locations of the security cameras. My hunch is he knows someone who works at Brighter Days, maybe more than one person."

"Why did the person bother with this build-up?" Finch asked. "Why bother with the break-ins at all? If he wants to attack someone, why doesn't he go ahead and do it?"

"One reason is that he wants to put fear into people's hearts," Reilly told them. "Scaring people is a power trip and that's part of his game plan ... in addition to him having a need to explain what he's doing and why. This is a person who won't be trifled with. He thinks he has a duty to keep order ... according to some master plan he's cooked up."

"Do you think the intruder will break into Brighter Days again?" Angie asked.

"I think he's made his point with the two break-ins. I think he'll move on to the next step."

"Which will be what?"

"The attack he has planned," Reilly said solemnly.

When the meeting was over, Reilly Henderson left the police station and Chief Martin had an evidence box brought into the conference room. The chief handed Finch a pair of surgical gloves.

Angie asked the older man, "Can we do anything to help?"

"If you and Miss Jenna could pull your chairs close to me, I believe having you both near would enhance my skills," Finch said.

The sisters' chairs made loud scraping noises as they moved over the floor to be positioned next to the man's seat.

"Would you like the lights turned off while you examine the bullet, Mr. Finch?"

"Thank you, Phillip, but that won't be necessary." Finch removed the bullet that had been left on the desk from the box and held it carefully in one hand. He closed his eyes.

Several minutes passed, and then Finch had the sensation of lifting from his chair and floating in a dark space. The man's breathing slowed and deepened. In his mind, he could see a blurry vision of the desk in the non-profit's small office as if he were watching from high above.

Someone stepped into the dark office. Finch could hear the scuff of the person's heavy boots.

The intruder's face was obscured by a hat, a mask, and the bulky coat's hood. The trespasser reached into one of the deep pockets of the coat and removed two items which were placed on the desk.

Handcuffs and a bullet.

Finch could feel the person's anger. He noticed the gloved hand tremble.

Terrible sensations ... hate, revenge, murderous rage ... floated on the air and threatened to smother Finch.

The person abruptly turned and stormed out of the office carrying a baseball bat in his hand.

Finch's eyes popped open. He sucked in a long breath, and then he quickly handed off the bullet to Chief Martin.

Angie and Jenna stood and put their arms around the older man.

"Are you okay, Mr. Finch?" Angie watched his face for signs of physical distress.

"I'm shaken, but fine." Finch's voice was soft.

Chief Martin brought him a cup of water and Finch gratefully sipped the cool liquid.

"I saw the person in the office."

"Could you see his face?" Jenna asked hopefully.

"I did not. The face was hidden." Finch explained what he saw and felt. "I wasn't sure if it was a man or a woman, but I would say it was a younger person, or maybe a middle-aged person. No older than that. He or she gave off deep, disturbing feelings. I believe the intruder intends to commit murder and I believe I know who he plans to target."

The older man rubbed at his eyes while Jenna, Angie, and the chief held their breaths.

Finch looked up at them with a weary expression. "I believe the intended victim is Beverly Tarant."

13

Everyone gathered in the kitchen to help make dinner and talk about the day's events. Mr. Finch and his girlfriend, Betty Hayes, stood at the counter and chopped vegetables for the salad.

"Are you sure you don't need to sit down, Victor? Your energy was drained by all the awful talk about that intruder and what he might do next." Betty gave a shudder. A successful Sweet Cove real estate agent, Betty did not know that the Roselands and Mr. Finch had paranormal powers. She *did* know they worked with the police on occasion to help solve difficult cases, but she was under the impression that their intellect and keen observation skills were the reasons they were such assets to law enforcement.

"I rested when we arrived home." Finch smiled and diced a carrot. "I'm fine now."

"Such a sweet man. How was I so lucky to find you?" Betty gave Finch a kiss on the cheek and his face flushed pink.

Jenna and Angie made eye contact and exchanged smiles. They loved that Mr. Finch had found a woman who doted on him and appreciated the wonderful person he was.

Courtney's boyfriend, Rufus, was making cookies with Ellie's boyfriend, Jack. Rufus said, "I didn't think old people were so lovey-dovey with each other."

Betty's eyes flashed at the young Englishman. "If I were you, I would be very careful who I called *old*."

"I didn't intend it to be an insult," Rufus said.

Betty held up her hand and sniffed. "Don't try to weasel your way out of it."

Finch said, "In truth, my dear, we are older, and there's nothing wrong with being older and wiser. In fact, in all my years, I've never been happier or more excited to be alive."

"This is why I love you, Victor." Betty batted her eyes at her boyfriend. "You are a prize."

Euclid and Circe trilled from their perch on top of the refrigerator.

"Tell us about the meeting with the psychologist," Tom said. He and Josh were working together to make a tomato sauce for the pasta.

Jenna, Angie, and Mr. Finch took turns filling in the family on what they learned from the meeting.

Ellie stood at the kitchen island preparing garlic bread. "So this person will attempt to kill someone next?"

No one said anything right away. Although they knew an attack on someone was imminent, nobody had put it so bluntly before and hearing someone say the words was sobering.

"That's what the psychologist believes will happen," Angie told them.

"Are you close to solving this mess?" Ellie's forehead creased with worry as she brushed olive oil over the bread slices.

"No," Angie admitted.

"But we know a lot of things," Courtney piped up with a reassuring tone in her voice. "We're probably closer to figuring it out than we think we are. We know the intruder probably knows someone who works at Brighter Days. The suspect believes he's morally superior to everyone else. He thinks it's his duty to maintain order. He's rule-based and feels it's his job to mete out punishment when someone breaks his rules."

Jenna added, "This person has probably been in the non-profit's offices before. He knew about the security cameras being there so he dressed in a way that hid any of his identifying features."

"The suspect believes he's powerful and important," Angie said. "The psychologist thinks he won't attempt another break-in at Brighter Days. She believes he'll escalate to the next level and attempt an attack on his intended victim."

"Sheesh," Rufus said. "How does the psychologist know all of this?"

"Dr. Henderson is well-educated and experienced in criminal profiling," Mr. Finch said.

Jack added some diced onions to the sauce pot. "Are the workers at the non-profit receiving police protection?"

Courtney shook her head. "There are too many employees to provide protection for all of them. Doing that would consume every resource the police have. Chief Martin and the chief from Silver Cove gave the Brighter Days's employees a class on ways to protect themselves. If the police knew who the target was, they'd offer that person some protection for a while, but they aren't sure who the victim might be. It's all speculation right now."

"Could the suspect be an employee of the non-profit?" Rufus asked.

"It's possible," Jenna said. "Chief Martin and the other officers have been interviewing the employees, but so far, no one stands out as a possible suspect. There's the woman who was fired for stealing, Joelle Young, and the chief is keeping her on the suspect list. She *did* steal from a colleague. She wasn't fired without cause, and she said she took full responsibility for the mistake. She doesn't sound like someone who would want revenge on anyone."

"What about motive?" Josh asked.

Angie lifted her hands in a helpless gesture. "We don't know. None of the workers claim to have had an argument or a run-in with anyone. Lydia, the director of the place, has some issues with her ex-husband, but when we spoke with him, he didn't seem to harbor hateful feelings."

"At least none he revealed," Courtney pointed out. "Our suspect is supposed to be able to control his anger ... *hide* his anger is probably a better way to say it. Lydia's husband could hold murderous thoughts about her, but is able to hide those feelings when necessary."

"Very good point, Miss Courtney," Finch praised the young woman.

"The tech manager, Bev Tarant, recently broke up with someone she'd been seeing for a short time," Angie said. "She and the man split amicably though."

When Betty and Rufus headed to the dining room with Ellie to set the table, Angie looked at Mr. Finch and nodded.

Finch said, "I had a vision today while holding the bullet left on the desk by the intruder."

All eyes turned to the man.

"What did you see?" Jack was fascinated by the family's paranormal skills.

Finch explained what he'd experienced. "The suspect is full of rage. He or she is boiling with hate and feelings of revenge. The sensations nearly smothered me."

Taking a quick look over her shoulder to be sure Betty or Rufus weren't coming back to the kitchen, Angie said, "Go ahead, Mr. Finch, tell them."

"What is it, Mr. Finch?" Josh asked.

"I think I know who the suspect's target will be."

Tom, Josh, and Jack's eyes widened.

"Who is it?" Tom questioned.

"I believe it is Beverly Tarant."

Euclid let out a wild hiss causing everyone to jump.

"Do you think the suspect is the man she broke up with?" Jack asked, after giving the cat a dirty look.

"We don't know. There really isn't any reason to think so," Jenna said. "Chief Martin is planning to interview Bev again tomorrow to find out if there's anyone she can think of who might wish to do her harm. And for now, the police are driving by her home at night every half-hour."

When dinner was over and the dishes cleared, Josh and Angie bundled up and decided to take a stroll around the neighborhood. They walked along the sidewalks hand in hand under the falling snow.

"Why is it snowing so much this year?" Angie shivered from the cold.

"To make us wish for summer," Josh kidded.

"Well, it's working on me. I wish all the time for warm weather. I like having snow for the holidays, but then I wish winter would go away and spring would arrive."

"When spring comes this year, there will be two

new additions in our family who will be almost two months old," Josh said.

"Has Tom slipped and told you if they're having a boy or a girl?" Angie asked.

Josh shook his head. "Tom hasn't slipped because he and Jenna don't know what they're having."

"You believe that?"

"Yeah, I do. If Jenna knew, she would have told you by now."

Angie nodded and then stuck her tongue out to catch a snowflake on it. "I guess they really do want a surprise."

"Do you have a feeling one way or the other? Are they having a boy or a girl?"

"I don't have a guess," Angie admitted. "Do you?"

"Not a clue. Does anyone have an idea about it?"

Angie said, "Courtney thinks they're having a girl. She said the babies will be born so close together that they'll be like twins ... just like me and Jenna."

Josh asked. "Do you feel your powers getting stronger? Orla said they'd increase with the birth of the babies."

"Right now, I feel like my powers are weaker. Jenna feels the same way. Orla told us that it's normal to experience that because all of our energy is going to the babies' development. It's after they're born when our powers will strengthen."

"That makes sense."

"Jenna and I worry we're going to miss something important with this investigation," Angie said. "I get flashes of feelings about the case, but mostly, I feel like I'm in a fog. I'm slower and less able to pick up on things. Jenna is feeling the same way. I'm glad we have Courtney and Mr. Finch to help."

"Ellie would help, too," Josh said.

"Yes, she would." Angie smiled. "But it would have to be one heck of an emergency for her to step in."

"If Tom or I can do anything to help, just say the word." Josh squeezed Angie's hand and chuckled. "I know we're good for nothing when it comes to the investigations, but I thought I'd offer in case there's something else I can do."

"Thanks," Angie said. "You never know. Maybe some of our powers will rub off on you someday."

"That's an interesting thought." Josh's eyes widened. "Is it possible?"

Angie slipped her arm through her husband's. "In this family, anything is possible."

14

The call from Chief Martin came in around midnight waking Angie and Josh who got up and woke Courtney and Mr. Finch. There had been a break-in at Lydia Hendricks's home while she slept. The chief asked if some of the family members might come to Lydia's house to listen in while he questioned her.

Courtney drove Finch and Angie to the woman's Colonial home where two police cars were parked in the driveway. Inside, Lydia and Chief Martin sat together in a downstairs room that was used as an office.

Looking frazzled and upset, Lydia clutched her robe around herself and greeted the Roseland sisters and Finch with words of appreciation.

"Thank you for coming so late at night. I'm sorry you were dragged out into the cold."

Finch took a seat next to the woman and said in a kind tone, "We're happy to help."

Chief Martin said, "We've gone over a few preliminary details together. There is a home security system, but it isn't functioning at the moment. The intruder broke a small pane of glass out of the backdoor and gained entry that way. The snow is packed down hard around the house and in the yard from all the cold weather we've had. It snowed earlier this evening, but there was a lot of wind and the new snow was blown away, so no footprints are visible." He looked at Lydia. "For the others' benefit, would you mind repeating what you've already told me?"

"I was sound asleep, but I stirred for some reason." Lydia's voice was heavy and thick. "Maybe I heard an unfamiliar noise. Maybe I heard the glass break. I don't know for sure. I became tense. I stayed perfectly still in my bed and listened. Something told me there was someone in the house." The woman's shoulders shook from recalling the late-night intrusion. "I heard movement downstairs. My bedroom door was open. I panicked. I was so afraid the person would come up to my room. I keep my phone on my nightstand. I grabbed it and tip-toed into the master bedroom. I locked the door and made the emergency call to the police."

Lydia's chest was rapidly rising and falling.

Angie noticed the signs of distress and said, "Why don't you take a break from the telling."

Lydia blinked fast. "No, thanks. I'd like to finish." She swallowed hard and kept going, wanting to be done with the explanation of the night's terror. "I heard someone enter my bedroom. I honestly thought I was going to have a heart attack. I sank onto the floor. Then I did something I didn't even think about. It was like some automatic response. I yelled through the door at the intruder. I told him to get out of my house. I told him the police were on their way. I yelled that I had a weapon." The corners of the woman's mouth turned up slightly for a second and she squared her shoulders. "The only weapons I had were a bottle of hairspray and a small pair of scissors, but if the person knocked the bathroom door in, I would have used both things to fight him off."

"Good for you," Courtney praised Lydia.

"What happened after you yelled at him?" Angie asked.

"I didn't hear anything. I wondered if he was

about to push the door in so I braced myself to act, but then I heard footsteps leaving the bedroom. My heart was racing like I've never felt before. I was sure he was going to get something he'd left downstairs to bash the door in, or maybe to call in an accomplice. I didn't dare leave the bathroom. I just waited. Every second seemed like an hour passing."

"Did the person come back?"

"He didn't. He must have left the house. The police arrived. I had given the dispatcher the code to open the garage door so the officers used it to gain entry. When I heard them downstairs, I ran from the bathroom." Lydia ran her hand over her hair. "I was afraid the intruder might be trying to trick me, but I'd seen the police car in the driveway from the bathroom window. I nearly collapsed into their arms, I was so happy to see them." Lydia's eyes misted over.

"Did the intruder speak?" Chief Martin asked. "Did you hear his voice?"

"He didn't say anything. All I heard were footsteps."

"Could you tell anything from the sound of the footsteps?"

"Like what? What could I tell?"

Not wanting to suggest anything she might have heard from the man walking inside the house, the chief asked, "Could you describe the sound of the footsteps?"

Lydia put a hand against the side of her face and looked down at the floor, thinking. "The sound was heavier than what you'd hear if someone was wearing everyday shoes like loafers or leather shoes. He must have had on boots, but the soles must have been softer because I heard a lighter step."

"Good," the chief said while hurriedly writing in his small notebook. "Excellent. Can you recall anything else?"

Lydia took in a deep breath. "I don't think the person was heavy or overweight. The footsteps were soft."

"Did it seem like the person was alone?" Finch asked. "Did you hear more than one set of footsteps?"

"I'm pretty sure he was alone." Lydia used both hands to brush at her eyes.

"Was anything taken from the house?" Courtney questioned. "Did he steal anything?"

"I took a quick look around when the officers arrived. I don't think anything was taken. Maybe he didn't have time. He might have heard my footsteps when I got out of bed and went into the bathroom.

Maybe he heard my voice as I called the police. That could be why he came upstairs."

"He was probably trying to decide if he had time to steal things or if he had to get out of the house right away," Courtney speculated.

Lydia looked at the chief, her face washed in worry. "Do you think this has to do with the break-in at the office? Do you think the intruder was after *me*?"

"It could be connected, I'm afraid."

"If the person intended to hurt Lydia, why would he run away before the police got here?" Courtney questioned. "The intruder left a bullet on the desk at the office. That tells me he has a gun." Courtney made eye contact with the woman. "I have to ask the next question and I apologize in advance for its bluntness." She turned back to Chief Martin. "Why didn't he shoot at the door's lock to get into the bathroom and then use the gun on Lydia? It wouldn't take long to do that. He had the time."

"He might have panicked," the chief said. "He might have been afraid that the police would arrive before he had time to complete his mission."

Lydia leaned her head back against the sofa.

"Can we get you something to drink?" Angie asked.

"I'd love a glass of water, if you don't mind." Lydia's face was white.

"Why don't we all take a few minutes break?" the chief suggested.

"I'll get the water for Lydia." Courtney helped Mr. Finch from the sofa and handed him his cane. "Why don't we get a drink, too."

"I'm going to stay here," Angie told them.

The chief, Courtney, and Finch left the room and headed for the kitchen.

With her head still resting against the back of the sofa, Lydia looked over at Angie. "I haven't asked you when you're due."

"Soon. About two or three weeks."

"What about your sister? Is she due around the same time?"

Angie said, "Our due dates are only days apart."

"How wonderful." A weak smile showed on the woman's face. "My boys are young men now. Everyone says it, but time surely does fly and kids are grown in the blink of an eye. Hold onto the time with your children with both hands. Don't let the moments slip away ... treasure them ... because once those moments are gone, you'll never get them back."

Angie held the woman's eyes and smiled at her.

Lydia blew out a breath of air. "Whoever thought my life would be like this? My marriage broken, me living alone in this big house, some nut terrorizing me and the employees. It's hard to believe."

"You did well during the break-in," Angie told Lydia. "You did all the right things. You kept your wits about you. You didn't panic. You're smart and brave."

"Thank you, but I sure didn't feel smart or brave at the time. I felt like a frenzied coward." Lydia's facial muscles looked less tense now.

Courtney came into the room carrying two glasses of water and she handed one to Lydia and one to Angie before taking a seat.

"Was there anything familiar about the sounds you heard during the break-in?" Courtney asked.

"Familiar how?" Lydia sipped her water.

"Did the person cough, mutter, say anything? Did the man's footsteps indicate anything familiar about his movements?"

When Lydia sat up, her face fell. "Oh. I know what you're getting at. You wonder if it was Roger who was in here."

Courtney nodded.

Lydia was quiet for a few moments. "I can't say for sure. The man didn't say anything. He didn't make any noises except for the sound of his footsteps. From hearing his steps, I wouldn't be able to say if it was Roger or not." She breathed a long breath. "I hope it wasn't him. How could I ever explain to our sons that their father was planning to kill me?"

15

"It looks like Lydia is the intended victim," Ellie said as they gathered after dinner around the fireplace in the living room with tea and strawberry scones.

Courtney looked over to Finch. "What are you thinking, Mr. Finch? You got the impression from your vision that the intruder was going to go after Bev Tarant, not Lydia Hendricks."

Circe was resting in the older man's lap as he stroked her fur. "I'm thinking that the target is Ms. Tarant."

"Last night's break-in at Lydia's house hasn't made you change your mind?" Angie asked.

"My sensations gave me information. Perhaps, they are wrong, but I haven't yet seen or heard enough to cause me to doubt what I felt."

Circe looked up at him and purred.

"Fair enough," Courtney said. "I would never doubt you."

"Do you think the break-in at Lydia's home is unrelated to the break-in at Brighter Days?" Jenna lifted her cup of tea to her lips.

"It very well could be," Finch replied.

"It would be quite a coincidence if the events weren't connected," Angie pondered the possibility. "But stranger things have happened."

"Who does everyone think broke in?" Ellie asked. "A random person, or was it Lydia's husband, Roger?"

"My money's on Roger." Courtney shifted the big orange cat in her lap a little to the side. "Have you put on weight, Euclid? You're crushing my leg."

Euclid lifted his head and scowled at the young woman.

"Why do you think it was Roger?" Finch asked.

"According to Lydia, Roger has been acting oddly," Courtney said. "He texts her all the time, he hangs out in the non-profit's parking lot waiting to see Lydia when she leaves work. He seems to be becoming more desperate and needy. He probably has no plan to kill her. Maybe he broke into the house in a miserable attempt to talk to Lydia. It was late, he might have been feeling lonely and despondent so he went to the house to try and speak with her. When he arrived, he discovered that the locks had been changed. Not thinking clearly, he broke a window to get in. When he heard Lydia walking around upstairs, he went to the second floor to see her. She yelled that she'd called the police. Roger froze. He snapped back to reality, realizing how stupid it was to break in, and then he ran away."

"It sure sounds like a plausible scenario," Angie agreed. "It would be a really dumb thing to do, but I understand how it could happen."

"I think you could be right about what happened," Ellie said. "But it could also have been a break-in completely unrelated to anything else. Someone may have known that Lydia lives in that big house all by herself. He may have wanted to steal things or maybe get a thrill from frightening her. I don't think the possibility should be dismissed, otherwise, you'll use your energy chasing after the wrong thing."

"Excellent points, Miss Ellie," Finch nodded.

"Maybe Chief Martin will have some news when he gets here," Angie said. "For now, why don't we look up Roger Hendricks and see what information we can find on him."

"Great idea." Ellie went to her office to get her laptop and returned to the living room with it. She began to tap on the keyboard. "Here he is. He's good-looking. He grew up in Connecticut, went to Yale for college, and graduated from Harvard Law School. He worked for hedge funds for a number of years, then joined the firm where he is currently a partner. The article mentions Lydia and the two sons. It reports the boards Roger is a member of, the charities he volunteers for, the donations he and Lydia have made to organizations in the area. It also mentions that he is an avid cyclist and, with his biking team, has raised over one million dollars for cancer research."

"Well," Courtney said. "He sounds like an upstanding citizen. Is there anything else?"

Ellie searched different articles and blogs until something she read caused her eyebrows to raise. "Listen to this. It's a blog that mentions Roger and his behavior in college. It accuses him of cheating, getting into fights, and stealing money that was raised by a group of his classmates for a charitable organization."

"Really?" Jenna leaned forward, and then giving it some thought, she said, "I guess it all could have been made up about him."

Ellie kept reading. "More than one person made the accusations, but nothing ever came of it. Nothing was proven. Roger was never formally accused and was never reprimanded in any way."

"It could all be lies about him," Angie said.

Courtney's eyes narrowed. "Or, it's all true, but Roger's daddy got him out of trouble by stepping in and taking care of it."

The family members groaned at the thought, but before they could discuss it any further, the doorbell rang, and Ellie went to greet Chief Martin and usher him to the living room.

"That fire sure feels good." The chief warmed his hands by the fireplace. "It's freezing outside, and it's snowing again."

Another groan was released by everyone.

Jenna poured some tea for the chief and Angie passed him the plate of scones.

"We've been speculating about who broke into Lydia's house," Jenna informed the law enforcement officer.

"Which way are the bets leaning?" Chief Martin bit into the strawberry scone.

"We haven't taken a formal poll," Courtney said, "but we have three scenarios. One, the person who broke-in at Brighter Days is targeting Lydia. Two,

Roger broke in just to talk with her and meant her no harm. I guess there are actually four scenarios. Three, Roger broke in with intent to kill Lydia. And four, it was some random person completely unrelated to anything at all who broke in."

"It seems you've covered all the bases." The chief added some honey to his tea.

"What do you think?" Finch asked. "Do you think one of our ideas is stronger than the others?"

"I'm going to reserve judgment, for now. I need more information," the chief said. "We've spoken with Roger Hendricks. He claims he was at home in bed when the intruder broke into Lydia's house."

Courtney made a face. "What else would he say?"

"Phone records report that Roger's phone was in his house," the chief said. "That doesn't mean Roger was at home, too. He might have left the phone at home and made a trip to Lydia's."

"He says he was alone that night?" Angie asked.

"So he says."

"Did he make any calls during the time of the break-in?"

"None."

"So who knows?" Jenna said. "He may or may not have been at home."

"I assume his car wasn't seen anywhere near Lydia's place?" Finch asked.

"It wasn't. Roger told us he left the car in the driveway. He didn't put it in the garage that night because he had the snow blower taken apart in there. Officers asked the neighbors if Roger's car was in the driveway. Two neighbors say it was there, but they went to bed early and couldn't be sure if the car was still there during the time period in question."

"Roger could have left the car in the driveway all night," Ellie pointed out. "But he's an avid cyclist. He could have ridden his bike to Lydia's."

"In the winter? In the snow?" Angie questioned.

"Cyclists ride their bikes in the winter," Ellie informed them. "Some put on different wheels with studs or ride fat bikes with wider tires."

"We'll ask around if anyone noticed a cyclist riding in the neighborhood late that night," Chief Martin said. "There's another development. Bev Tarant contacted me a little while ago."

A rush of anxiety flooded Angie's veins.

The chief said, "The man she'd been dating, Allen Poulin, texted and called her several times today. It took her by surprise that he communicated. She hadn't seen or heard from him for a couple of weeks. They agreed to no longer date and each of them was fine with the decision. When Bev saw the call from Allen, she was concerned something had happened so she answered. He told her he'd made a mistake and he wanted to continue to see her. She didn't agree that it was a good idea and told him she wasn't open to seeing him again. Allen became belligerent so Bev ended the call. Allen called twice more, but she wouldn't pick up. He texted her five times. Each message became more insulting. Bev blocked his number."

"What happened to make him change his mind and want to see her again?" Courtney asked. "Did he tell Bev why?"

"He only said he'd made a mistake," Chief Martin said.

"Did he sound drunk?" Jenna asked.

"Bev didn't report thinking he'd had too much to drink."

"Did Allen mention anything going on in his life that might have influenced him needing to be with Ms. Tarant?" Finch asked. "Had he been laid off? Did he lose a friend or family member? Was he in a bad accident? Emotional stresses often push people towards someone who might be able to comfort them."

"That's a good point," the chief said. "Bev didn't mention anything like that. I'll ask her about it."

"The calls and texts must be concerning to Bev," Angie said. "Allen never acted like this before, right?"

"He didn't."

"Is she worried about him?"

"Bev is baffled by the behavior," the chief said. "She hopes Allen hasn't fallen into a depression or a state of anxiety. She told me she encouraged him to go see his doctor, but he only swore at her for suggesting such a thing."

"This case is taking some weird turns." Courtney scratched Euclid's neck.

Angie sighed. "And those turns aren't making anything easier."

16

"This will be the last game night before the babies are born," Jenna pointed out.

"We'd better enjoy tonight then," Angie kidded as she checked the Pastitsio, a pasta, meat, tomato sauce, and béchamel sauce dish, baking in the oven.

"Why are there *two* baby high chairs set up in here?" Rufus asked. "Jenna doesn't live here."

"She may not live here, but she's here all the time," Courtney said with a smile. "Anyway we need two of everything because Orla and Mr. Finch are going to babysit here in the Victorian."

Ellie had made a stew called spetsofai which had country sausages, green peppers, onions, and wine. There was also a vegetarian stew called fasolakia with green beans, potatoes, and tomato sauce. "The stews are ready. I turned the pots down to keep them warm."

Pita bread, hummus, olives, and chunks of feta cheese were set out on the kitchen island for appetizers. After finishing up making the baklava, Courtney was helping get everyone a drink as the group mingled in the kitchen talking. The break-in at Lydia's house had been the main topic of conversation and guesses were being made about who the perpetrator might be.

"I bet it was some guy who lives in Lydia's neighborhood." Rufus put some olives and hummus onto his small plate. "He was probably hoping he could steal some money or a laptop."

"If he wanted to steal things, why would he go upstairs and risk coming face to face with the homeowner?" Courtney handed Rufus a glass of wine.

"Maybe he couldn't find anything worthwhile on the first floor." Rufus shrugged. "Lydia probably scared him when she shouted about calling the police from the bathroom and he took off."

"I think it was her ex-husband, Roger," Courtney offered her opinion. "I think he was alone and despondent so he decided to go to Lydia's house to see if she'd talk to him. When he heard she'd called the police, he got frightened and ran."

"Do you think Roger is the one who broke-in at the non-profit?" Ellie asked.

"I'm not sure about that." Courtney dipped a piece of pita bread into the small scoop of hummus on her plate. "Roger *could* be the intruder, or he might not be connected to the non-profit's break-in at all and he just turned up at Lydia's place to talk, with no intention of hurting her."

"Do you still think Bev Tarant is the target?" Tom asked.

"I think she might be," Courtney said, making eye contact with Mr. Finch.

"Why do you think she's the target?" Betty Hayes asked. "Because the bullet was left on her desk?"

"Partly that, and partly for no reason other than that's my guess. It's how I feel."

"Evidence is needed," Betty huffed. "Not guesses or feelings."

Courtney shared a little smile with Finch. Betty had not been told about their paranormal powers so Courtney was unable to point to Mr. Finch's vision as evidence.

Chief Martin arrived with his wife, Lucille, carrying a big bowl of rice, a bowl of salad, and a platter of Greek butter cookies. The shoulders of their coats were covered with snowflakes.

The couple had only been in the kitchen for a minute before Betty asked the chief what was new on the case. Chief Martin looked weary and tired and gratefully accepted a beer from Courtney.

"The chief needs a break," Courtney said. "He needs time to unwind and enjoy himself away from the pressure of the case. The brain needs time to subconsciously ponder the clues. I think tonight we should have a ban on talking about the non-profit break-ins and the break-in at Lydia's house."

Chief Martin looked at Betty. "There really isn't anything new. We've been talking to people involved in the case. So far, nothing important has come up."

"You'll figure it out, Phillip," Betty said. "We all have great faith in you."

Euclid and Circe trilled their agreement from atop of the refrigerator.

The group moved into the dining room to enjoy the meal, and much praise was heaped on the chefs for creating the delicious food.

Lucille passed a bottle of seltzer to Angie who poured it into her and Jenna's glasses.

"How are you both feeling?" Lucille asked the young women.

"We're pretty uncomfortable," Jenna admitted. "Neither one us can sleep through the night now. It's hard to find a good position to sleep in, the babies are always kicking, and we have to visit the bathroom all the time."

Lucille smiled. "It reminds me of my pregnancies. I think we become so uncomfortable in the ninth month that when labor starts we're actually happy to face it."

"I don't have to get up as early as Angie does for the bake shop so I feel guilty if I complain about feeling tired," Jenna said. "And she's on her feet all day, too."

"But my day is over at 4pm while you work at least until 6pm or 7pm," Angie told her sister.

"I like my schedule better," Jenna said. "I'm not naturally an early morning person." She chuckled. "At least I won't be for another week or so, then the baby will have me up bright and early every day."

After desserts, coffees, and teas were served and consumed, the table was cleared for the games. Josh, Tom, Finch, and Rufus prepared for the cut-throat card game with each one trash-talking the others. Ellie, Jack, Chief Martin, and Lucille got out a word game and settled at the card table to play while Angie, Betty, Jenna, and Courtney played charades in the living room where a fire was burning in the fireplace.

Euclid and Circe rested on the rug in front of the fire.

After an hour of play, Angie took a break and headed for the kitchen for a cold drink. Chief Martin came in right after her.

"How are you feeling?" he asked.

Angie gave him a short list of her physical complaints, and then laughed. "I bet you were expecting me to say everything was great."

The chief gave her a smile. "If men had to carry and deliver children, the human race would go extinct. I'm surprised your list of physical issues isn't longer."

"I only gave you the condensed version," Angie grinned and handed the chief a glass of seltzer with a slice of lime. "How are you holding up with this case?"

"I'm tired. Maybe the gray skies and the cold, snowy weather is having an influence on my energy levels."

"The winter does that to me, too. It goes on far too long for my taste."

"I worry that we're missing something," the chief said. "I don't like the change in personality that Allen Poulin exhibited to Bev."

"Maybe he was drunk," Angie guessed. "The

alcohol made him feel depressed and he called Bev and ended up ranting. Allen probably doesn't even remember he talked to her."

"That could be. What about Roger Hendricks? Are we missing something with him?"

"His behavior with Lydia is over the top," Angie said. "Whining, badgering her, and showing up unannounced outside her office makes him seem pathetic. If he wants to get back together with her, he's not doing a very good job of showing his best side. Why not send her flowers, or write her a heart-felt letter? I don't know. She told me he never even apologized for cheating on her. He could start with that. What he's doing is only going to push her away, not draw her to him."

"He's probably fallen into desperation and isn't thinking straight," the chief said.

"Then he can kiss goodbye any opportunity he might have had to get a second chance with Lydia. It seems he's digging his own grave." Angie made a face. "Why did that sentence send a creepy feeling through my body?"

"It's only a figure of speech. I hope." The chief took a long drink of his seltzer. "Are we missing something about the people we interviewed at the non-profit? Is there a suspect hidden in the group of people who work there? Is someone at Brighter Days the perpetrator?"

"Maybe we should talk to some of them again. Things aren't falling into place. We barely have any suspects at all," Angie said.

"Mr. Finch thinks Bev is the perp's intended victim," the chief said. "Is that reason enough to try and give her police protection? How would I justify it to my superior? I can't tell them Mr. Finch had a vision and I believe in his paranormal skills."

"Can you say it's because the bullet and hand-cuffs were on Bev's desk? Would that be enough reason to provide protection?"

"Probably not." Chief Martin sighed and he ran his hand over his face. "If anything happens to Bev...." He let his voice trail off.

"We'll figure it out. We always have setbacks. We'll find the answers we need."

The chief's phone buzzed in his pocket and when he read the message, his face tightened. "There's been a break-in at Monica Windsor's house."

"Oh, no." Angie's eyes went wide. "Is she okay? Is her family okay?"

"I don't have any more information. I need to get over there."

"First, a break-in at Lydia's and now, a break-in at Monica's. What the heck is going on?"

"I have no idea." Chief Martin looked at Angie. "Can you come? Can a couple of the others come? If you're not up to it, it's okay. I understand."

"I'm going with you. I'll get my coat." Angie started out of the kitchen. "I'll ask some of the others to come, too. I guess game night has just come to an abrupt end."

17

Angie, Courtney, and Chief Martin hurried into Monica Windsor's house to find an officer talking with her and she looked relieved to see them.

"I've never been so frightened in my life." Her hair held back in a ponytail, Monica wore red flannel pajamas and fluffy socks. Her face was an odd mix of exhaustion and intensity. "I almost had a heart attack."

Chief Martin ushered the woman into her living room and then asked the other officer to take a look outside for footprints or for any other clues. A second officer was speaking with Monica's husband in the dining room.

Chief Martin spoke with a gentle voice. "I know you've been telling the officer what happened, but we'd like to hear the information directly from you. Do you need a few minutes to rest or have some coffee?"

"I'm okay, just shook up. I can tell you about it." Monica leaned back against the sofa for a few seconds, and then quickly sat up straight as if she'd suddenly collected herself and was now determined to tell about the incident despite the toll it had taken on her. "Ted and the kids left about 6pm to visit his mother. I have a cold and I didn't think I should go. I didn't want to spread it to my mother-in-law so I stayed home. They had dinner together at her house and the kids were going to stay overnight with her. Ted was planning to be home a little after 11pm. I ate some soup and then I worked for a few hours at the dining room table. I was behind on some things and wanted to get caught up in case my cold got worse and I needed to take a day off from work."

Chief Martin nodded, but didn't ask anything so that Monica would tell the tale in her own way.

"I got tired. I made up a cup of tea and came in here. I was sitting on the other sofa." She pointed to the one Angie and Courtney were on. "I decided to lay down for a few minutes. I fell asleep." Monica's shoulders shook. "When I woke up, the one light that was on is attached to a timer and it had gone out. The room was dark, but the kitchen light was on and shined a little into this room." The woman's hand went to her throat. "Have you ever had that sensation where you've been asleep and you wake up and you have the feeling of certainty that someone is in the room? It's happened when our kids were little and they came into the bedroom in the middle of night. Well, I *knew* someone was in the living room with me. I could *feel* him standing just a few yards away."

"It was a man?" Courtney asked.

Monica nodded. "I didn't move. I knew it wasn't Ted. My mind was racing. What was I going to do? What did he want? Was he here to kill me?"

Angie's stomach was in knots listening to the story.

"I decided I wasn't going to lie there waiting for his attack. I leapt to my feet and made a run for the kitchen. I think I surprised the man when I jumped up because he seemed to hesitate. But then I felt his hand on my shoulder. He yanked me back, but I kept my balance. I kicked him and scratched him and I punched him in the face."

Angie and Courtney both smiled at Monica's self-defense.

"I wasn't going down without a fight." Monica

rubbed the knuckles on her right hand. "I thought earlier that I might have broken my hand. I think it's just bruised."

"Good for you. It's great that you fought back," the chief said encouragingly.

"Did the man back down?" Angie asked.

"No, he didn't. We both fell to the floor. I can't remember every detail, but I pulled on the side table and the lamp tipped off and I think it hit him in the head. I scrambled away on my hands and knees, got up, and dashed into the kitchen. I grabbed a knife from the drawer and spun around to face him. Just then I heard the garage door going up. Ted was home." Relief washed over Monica's face at the thought. "I screamed to him. I don't remember what I yelled, but Ted heard how frantic I sounded. He dashed in through the kitchen door."

"Did Ted chase the intruder from the house?" Angie asked.

Monica shook her head. "The guy must have heard the garage door, too. He took off. He ran out the back." She gestured to the door leading to the outside from the kitchen.

"Can you describe the man?" Chief Martin asked.

"Not much. It was dark in here. I couldn't see

much of anything. He was wearing a winter coat. He had on a ski mask. His hood was up. He wore gloves. Not heavy ones, thin kitted ones."

"Did he say anything to you?" Courtney questioned.

"Nothing. Not a word. He did grunt when I punched him." Monica looked proud of that.

Chief Martin asked, "Was there anything about him that seemed familiar?"

"No. I was so freaked out by it all, I don't think I would have recognized my own brother if he was standing in here. All I wanted was to get away from him." Monica looked down at the cuts on her knuckles. "I'm ashamed to say it, but when he put his hand on my shoulder and yanked me around, all I wanted to do was kill him."

"Don't be ashamed," Angie said. "You were fighting for your life. He came into your home and attacked you. Don't be ashamed of wanting to live ... or for fighting hard."

Monica's eyes teared up and she brushed at them. "All I could think of was my kids and Ted. I didn't want my kids to grow up without a mother. I didn't want to leave Ted alone. I *did* fight hard ... for me and my family."

Angie's throat tightened with emotion.

Monica looked to the chief. "Do you think this man is the same person who attacked Lydia?"

"It seems to be the case, although I won't say with certainty until we've investigated."

"Are we *both* the intruder's targets?" Worry tugged at the corners of Monica's eyes. "Is there more than one person he's after? Is he after *me* and Lydia?"

"It's possible," the chief said.

Monica fell back against the sofa and covered her eyes with her hand. "My kids. I can't put my kids in danger. I should move to a hotel room or an apartment temporarily."

Ted came into the room and took a seat next to his wife. "You won't be going anywhere without me."

Monica took his hand and rested her head against his shoulder. "What a terrible mess."

Courtney and Angie shared a quick look. Their eyes were filled with determination to find the person terrorizing these people.

"Did you catch a glimpse of the intruder?" Chief Martin asked Ted.

"I didn't. He was out the door by the time I came in from the garage. The backdoor was open and Monica was standing by the sink with a knife in her hand." Ted's face hardened. "I wish he *was* still in the kitchen when I came in. There would have been a royal battle in here."

Angie didn't doubt it. She could see the anger on Ted's face.

"It was a violation," Ted said. "Someone broke into our home and tried to hurt Monica." The man's expression changed to one of sudden realization. "That guy must have been watching the house. He must have seen me and the kids drive away. He must have waited and broke in when he didn't see Monica moving around inside. He must have assumed she was watching television or taking a nap." Ted's hands balled into fists. "He's been watching us."

Monica's eyes widened. "Is Lydia okay? Did anyone check on Lydia or Bev?"

The chief said, "We've had squad cars go to their homes to check on them. They're both fine. Nothing unusual has happened at either home this evening. Officers will be stationed outside their houses all night. The same for you two. A car will be out front until morning."

"Thank you," Ted said gratefully.

"In light of what happened and in retrospect, had you noticed anyone suspicious around the neighborhood recently?" the chief asked. "Maybe someone you ignored initially, but now, thinking back, recall someone in the neighborhood who you didn't recognize?"

Monica and Ted looked at one another.

"I can't think of anyone," Ted said.

Monica shook her head.

"What about a car that was unfamiliar?"

"I didn't notice one," Monica said.

Ted hadn't seen anything suspicious either.

"Did you receive any unusual phone calls?" the chief asked.

"No, we didn't," Monica told him.

"Did you notice that man around who harassed you the other evening outside of the non-profit's office?"

"We haven't seen him since that night," Ted reported.

"Should we move away?" Monica directed the question to Chief Martin.

The chief said kindly, "I wouldn't advise you one way or the other. The officers are outside searching for clues. The team is dusting for fingerprints. Clues and leads can appear at any moment, sometimes when they're least expected. Take a few days. Let us process the information. This man will make a mistake."

Monica's face showed skepticism about what the

chief was saying. Someone had broken into their home. Someone had attacked her. It would take some time for her to feel safe in her house again.

"An EMT is here," the chief said. "Let's have her look at your hand. It might be a good idea to go to the hospital for an x-ray."

Ted nodded and put his arm around his wife's shoulders. "Let's do that. And then let's pack some bags and go to my mother's house in the morning. We can stay there for a few days and process what's happened."

Angie thought that was a very smart idea.

18

The sun had nearly set when Angie and Jenna parked the car in the Sweet Cove resort's lot and walked over the hard-packed snow to Robin's Point, a spot that meant so much to their family. As little kids, the Roseland sisters spent happy summers at the Point at their nana's cottage until a problem with the land resulted in her losing her cozy, little house.

Josh and his brother eventually purchased the land and had the elegant Sweet Cove resort built on it. When Josh met Angie and fell in love with her, he bought out his brother's ownership share in the resort, and had a lawyer draw up papers that returned most of Robin's Point to the Roseland sisters with each one receiving a plot of land. None of them had built on it, and they weren't sure if they ever would.

Angie and her sisters always felt close to their nana whenever they were on the Point and she and Jenna felt the urge to walk over to the bluff despite the cold and biting wind.

"Maybe we shouldn't have walked over here," Jenna laughed as the wind almost whipped her hat from her head.

Angie pulled her scarf higher on her neck and kidded, "We better not get blown off the bluff."

"That would be impossible," Jenna joked, "we both weigh too much now. We're like anchors hugging the land."

They stood on the cliffs high above the sea watching the waves crash on the beach below where some snow and ice covered part of the sand.

"It's dramatic, isn't it?" Jenna asked, slipping her arm through Angie's. "The waves are huge."

A seagull flew high overhead and they could hear its high-pitched call.

"I heard they're predicting a big storm for next week. A foot of snow is possible," Angie told her sister.

Jenna groaned. "Like we need more snow. It seems like it's been snowing non-stop this winter.

The babies better not decide to come in the middle of a blizzard."

Angie felt a shiver of nervousness run over her skin. "Have you seen Nana's ghost recently?"

"No. I feel her around when I'm in the jewelry shop, but she hasn't shown herself for a while. You know how she is. She has a mind of her own."

Angie smiled. "I think that trait of hers was passed on to all of us."

"Do you feel her?" Jenna asked.

"Every time I'm here I can feel her in my blood."

"Me, too. It feels nice, cozy and warm, like she has her arms wrapped around me."

"Yeah." Angie had the same sensation. She especially needed to feel her grandmother's love whenever they worked a difficult case. She needed the closeness and the connection between them to give her the strength and courage to keep going, to not give up, to believe they could find the answers to what they were looking for. With a sigh, she asked, "Are you frozen yet? Want to head home?"

"A cup of tea and a nice fire sounds pretty good to me right now," Jenna said. "Race you to the car?"

Angie chuckled. "As long as it's a walking race."

$\sim$

When the sisters arrived at the Victorian, they entered the kitchen through the backdoor to see Courtney sitting at the table reading. When she heard her sisters coming in, she slipped the book to the side of the table and closed it.

Euclid and Circe jumped down off the fridge to greet the young women.

"We stopped at Robin's Point." Jenna hung her coat on the peg on the wall.

"How was it?" Courtney asked.

"Freezing." Angie put the tea kettle on the stove. "What are you reading?"

"Nothing much."

Angie stared at her youngest sister. "There's a book in front of you, but it's nothing much?"

"It's just a book." Courtney tried to change the subject. "Why were you at the Point?"

"We needed to connect with Nana." Jenna put some cookies on a plate and carried it to the table.

Angie filled cups with tea and brought one over to Courtney, taking a glance at the book she seemed to be trying to hide.

"Childbirth?" Angie asked with surprise. "You're reading a book on childbirth?"

"So what?" Courtney poured cream into her cup and took a cookie from the plate.

Angie stared. "Is something going on?"

"Like what?" Courtney shifted nervously in her chair.

"Like why are you reading about childbirth?"

Courtney gave her sister a look like she was thick in the head. "Because my two sisters are about to give birth. I'd like to know more about it."

"Why?" Jenna had become suspicious, too.

"For Pete's sake. I don't need an ulterior motive."

Mr. Finch came in leaning on his cane. "I thought I heard you all talking in here."

"Will you tell these two to stop giving me the third degree?" Courtney asked Finch for help.

"What is the inquisition about?"

Angie carried over a cup of tea for the man.

"This book I'm reading." Courtney gestured to it.

"Ah. The childbirth book. I read it last week. Ellie, too." Finch sipped the hot liquid in his cup.

"Why?" Angie demanded. "Why are you all so interested in the birth process?"

Finch and Courtney made eye contact.

Finch said, "Should either of you need assistance during labor and delivery, we will be here to help you."

"We'll be at the hospital," Jenna said with a grin. "Maybe the nurses and the doctors will let you help them." She was about to walk to the kitchen island, when she stopped and slowly turned around. "Wait a second. Do you two have some *feeling* about us giving birth?"

"What do you mean?" Courtney asked.

"You know what I mean," Jenna was growing impatient. "Is something wrong?"

Finch said, "It's been a snowy winter."

Angie folded her arms on the table and said very slowly, "Okay, you both need to spill what you know."

"We don't know anything," Courtney said, looking away.

When Angie and Jenna turned their eyes on Mr. Finch, Euclid let out a hiss.

Finch looked up at the cat who was back on his perch on top of the refrigerator. "The big orange boy doesn't like it when we aren't upfront with you."

Angie sighed, "Finally." She turned to Euclid. "Thanks, good boy."

Finch said, "Courtney and I had some feelings. We discussed them and we thought we should learn about childbirth."

"What sort of feelings?" Jenna asked. "Tell us."

"Just mild worries," Finch said reassuringly. "Nothing upsetting. It's been very snowy. The roads are often slippery. We thought ... what if you can't make it to the hospital? What if the snow prevents medical help from reaching the Victorian? Women have delivered babies on their own, without doctors, for thousands of years. We thought we'd learn about the process in case you need to have a home birth."

"We're going to have home births?" Angie asked. "You both sensed this?"

"No, no," Finch said. "It wasn't a vision or anything, Miss Angie. Just fleeting thoughts." The man smiled. "It never hurts to be prepared."

Courtney said, "See. That's all it is. We're taking our jobs as family members seriously. If you need us, we'll be ready."

Circe trilled.

"Okay," Jenna said. "I'm going to hope we won't need you, but it's very nice of the three of you to learn how to help. We appreciate it."

Angie nodded.

"We didn't want to mention it because we knew you'd both freak out," Courtney said. "So we read when you aren't around."

"There's probably a couple weeks before the babies arrive," Jenna pointed out. "That's enough time for you to intern in the hospital delivery room.

Why don't you call them and ask them if you can practice there?"

"Very funny," Courtney huffed. "We're taking this seriously. When you go into labor and can't get to the hospital, you'll be sorry you were so sassy with us. We'll only help Angie."

Ellie came into the kitchen, her long blond hair swinging behind her back. "I'll help you, Jenna, but you have to be extra nice to me for the next two weeks. You can start by helping me put out the pre-dinner beverages and appetizers for the bed and breakfast guests."

"You'd better do it," Courtney advised. "You've made enemies of me and Mr. Finch."

Jenna rolled her eyes while Angie laughed.

"I should be the one getting waited on and treated nicely. I'm about to have a baby."

Courtney said, "I read in the childbirth book that women who are active and fit, in general, have an easier delivery than other women."

"Come on," Ellie encouraged. "You help me, and when the time comes, I'll help you."

Jenna groaned and stood up to help put out the late afternoon snacks. "I don't know why you're all being so mean to me."

"It's because we love you." Courtney opened the

childbirth book to where she'd left off. "I'm glad I don't have to sneak around anymore to read this thing."

Angie leaned close to Mr. Finch. "Would you suggest that when our contractions start, we should head to the hospital right away?"

"I would." Finch nodded. "You never know when a sudden storm might arise. And you certainly don't want to get stuck on the roads and not be able to make it to the hospital."

"Suggestion taken." Angie smiled at their adopted family member. "I think I'll be watching the weather very closely over the next two weeks or so."

"So will I, Miss Angie. So will I."

19

It was just before midnight when a Silver Cove police officer sat in his car at the curb in front of Bev Tarant's ranch house with the engine running. Light snow was falling and the little flakes sparkled in the light of the streetlamp.

Someone tapped on the driver's side window startling the young officer who straightened in his seat and pushed the button to slide the window down.

That was a mistake.

In a swift movement, the person who had knocked on the window reached out and sliced the officer's neck. Blood spurted, and in minutes the young cop was dead.

When this was going on, Bev was sound asleep

in the master bedroom. The house was quiet and dark. She had no roommates ... and no pets to warn her that someone was coming.

It was easy for the person to break in. The back-door lock was a piece of trash that wasn't worth the money it cost to purchase it. It took less than forty seconds and the person was inside the house standing in the kitchen in the dark.

There was a squeaky spot on the wood floor and when the intruder stepped on it, the sound of the squeak was loud in the quiet house, and it caused Bev to stir.

The woman opened one eye and looked at the clock on her bedside table. Relieved that she still had six more hours to sleep, Bev turned over, but instead of dozing off, she froze.

Was that a footstep?

Was someone in the house?

Bev slipped out of bed. She grabbed the pepper spray from the side table and the hammer she kept on her headboard. She didn't want to be caught with nothing to use to fight back with. The Brighter Days intruder scared her, and some nights she couldn't sleep, thinking about what she would do if he came to her house looking for her.

Bev's heart pounded and sweat trickled down her back.

She heard a footstep in the hallway, and she flung herself out of the bedroom and ran down the hall to meet the trespasser.

The hammer struck the person on the shoulder, but when Bev pressed the button on the canister of pepper spray, the fluid went wide and missed its mark.

The intruder had a stun gun and attempted to us it on Bev, but she moved to the side and it only glanced her arm. Bev hit the person with the hammer and made contact, but she couldn't tell where the blow had landed. The attacker punched the young woman in the head and Bev stumbled. She bashed the hammer into the person's leg just as he hit her in the face. They continued to fight ... Bev knew it was the fight of her life.

The hammer almost fell from her hand, but she managed to keep it in her grasp.

The next blow she landed cracked a bone ... maybe a bone in the intruder's hand.

The attacker slashed Bev's arm with his knife, pushed her, and then turned and ran from the house.

Bev sank to the floor to catch her breath, then

she was up on her feet in a few seconds. She flicked on the light and looked for her phone on the kitchen island. It wasn't there.

Tears flowed from her eyes as she ran into the bathroom to get a hand towel to wrap around her bleeding arm. She grabbed her car keys and rushed for the garage and into her car. In ten minutes, she was at the Silver Cove police station.

Angie was once again awoken by her phone buzzing. After speaking with Chief Martin, she woke Courtney, and they drove to meet the chief at the area hospital.

"The officer is dead. He was watching the house from the squad car. Someone attacked him. He bled out." The chief's face was white and perspiration showed on his forehead.

Angie couldn't keep a gasp from escaping from her throat. Courtney held her sister's arm.

"Officers and investigators are at Bev's house. We think the attacker took Bev's phone. A bag was found on the kitchen floor. It contained handcuffs, two knives, a stun gun, rope, and a handgun."

"Bev?" Angie asked. "Is she...?"

"She's okay. She needed stitches for a knife wound on her arm and her face is swollen and bruised from taking blows. We can go in to see her now."

Bev was resting on her back in the hospital bed. One of her eyes was half-closed from the swelling. Her cheek was already black and blue and swollen.

"I'm okay," Bev's voice croaked. "The attacker ran from the house."

Chief Martin, Angie, and Courtney pulled chairs over to the bedside.

"You're amazing," Angie said. "You're brave and strong. You fought hard."

"I'm really not. My survival instinct kicked in. I wasn't thinking, just acting." Bev took in a long breath and released it slowly. "I think I did some damage to him."

"Are you able to tell us what happened?" the chief asked.

"Yes." Bev started the tale from the moment she stirred in her bed. "I heard the kitchen floor squeak. I knew someone was in the house. I knew he was in the kitchen. I know that squeak well." She paused for a moment and then went on. "I got out of bed, grabbed my pepper spray and hammer." Bev explained why she kept the two things by her bed.

"That was smart," Courtney praised her.

"I heard another footstep and decided to go after him before he could attack me. We met in the hallway." Bev closed her eyes for several seconds. "I flailed. I was like a banshee. I didn't care what I hit as long as I hit somewhere on his body. I just kept striking out at him. My adrenaline was racing. I really didn't feel the blows he landed. Well, maybe I did, but they didn't stop me."

"He ran?"

Bev nodded and then grimaced from the pain when she moved her neck. "He did. I think I got him good with the hammer. I tried to find my phone to call for help, but I couldn't find it so I ran to the car and drove to the police station. They called an ambulance and took me here."

"Did you see the attacker's face?"

"He was wearing a mask. He had on a hood, a bulky jacket. There were gloves on his hands. He was basically wearing what he wore in the security tapes. I couldn't see his face at all."

"Did the person say anything to you?"

"No, nothing."

"Did he grunt or moan?"

"Yeah." Bev's eyes narrowed. "I think so. Maybe it was me."

"Did the grunts sound like a man?"

"They might have." Bev rubbed at her wrist. "Maybe. I can't be sure. I'm sorry. Maybe I'll remember more later."

"Did the person seem familiar?"

Bev tilted her head slightly. "At first, I thought it might be Allen. Then I had a moment when I thought it might be Joelle Young."

"Why did you think it was Joelle?" Angie asked.

"The person seemed very strong. For an instant, the impression I had was that it was Joelle. The idea just popped into my mind. But I also had moments when I thought it was Allen. I'm so confused. I don't know for sure." Bev looked exhausted as she rested her head back on the pillow. "I heard a nurse and an officer talking. One of them said the officer outside my house was dead. Is it true?"

No one answered.

"Tell me. Is it true? Did the officer assigned to watch my house get killed?"

Chief Martin cleared his throat. "He was attacked. He didn't make it."

"Oh, no. I'm so sorry this happened." A tear slipped down Bev's cheek. "Why? Why is this person doing all of this? He didn't have to kill that officer." Bev looked at the chief. "When I ran from the house to the car, I stumbled over a small duffle bag on the floor. I didn't stop to see what was in it. Did anyone find it in the kitchen?"

"Yes. It seems the bag belonged to the intruder."

"Was there anything in it?" Bev asked.

"A few things." The chief told her the contents of the bag and she visibly paled.

"He was going to kill me, that's for sure." Bev's voice was a whisper. "Why is he targeting us? What did we do to him? Do I know him? Or her?"

"The house is being fully processed," the chief told her. "There will be a clue. He'll make a mistake."

Bev's lower lip trembled. "But will the mistake be found when he finally succeeds in killing one of us? How long can this go on?"

"The intruder is becoming bolder," Angie said. "He'll slip up. He'll leave a clue. And then the police will arrest him."

"I don't know how I can ever feel safe in my house again. I don't think I can. I'll have to put it on the market. I can't keep it." Bev shuddered.

"Wait a little while," Chief Martin suggested. "Don't act in haste. Move out for a bit and then reassess when things have settled down."

"I don't know if I can do that." Bev passed her hand over her eyes. "Maybe I should get a dog."

"Don't make any decisions yet," Angie said gently. "Give yourself time to think things over. Give yourself time to recover from the fight you had in your kitchen."

"I guess so. I'll have to move out though. I can't stay there right now. I can't even imagine going back there."

"Do you have someone you can stay with?" Angie asked.

Bev nodded. "I'll call my close friend. She has an extra bedroom." Letting out a long, drawn-out sigh, she added, "What a terrible, terrible mess."

20

It was late afternoon and Angie was busy closing up the museum bake shop when Chief Martin came up to the counter.

"I was driving by and knew you were working here today. Do you have time to chat?" Chief Martin asked.

"Sure. Everything's almost done for the day." Angie set down the kitchen towel she'd been cleaning the countertops with. "Cup of coffee?"

"That's music to my ears." The chief sank down onto one of the café chairs and Angie, carrying a cup of coffee, came over to sit with him.

"I'd ask if there was good news, but your facial expression doesn't match up with telling me anything positive."

"You're right. I don't have any good news. I wish I did." The chief took a long drink from his cup. "I *did* interview someone who previously employed Joelle Young. He had a few things to say."

Angie leaned forward a little. "Tell me."

"Joelle was stealing small amounts from the company."

Angie's eyes went wide. "Was she? So the stealing at Brighter Days wasn't anything new."

"Seems not. The man I spoke with owns a car dealership. His name is Alex Jonas. Joelle was hired as the bookkeeper and accountant. Over time, they became suspicious that she might be stealing from the company. An accountant who was a friend of Jonas's took a look at the books and found discrepancies. He suggested the owner notify the police. Jonas didn't want to do that. He said Joelle was fresh out the military and he didn't want her to have a difficult re-entry into civilian life. He thought she should have a second chance. Now, he regrets that decision. He told me if he'd contacted police and filed against Joelle, it would have saved another company from suffering losses like his did. Jonas thinks Joelle might have an addictive personality. She likes to gamble. She puts up a good front that she's just a casual gambler, but Jonas said there's every sign that she's addicted to gambling and is losing a good deal of her money. She needs help. He suggested she see a counselor, but she rebuffed the idea."

"I understand why the guy feels badly. Joelle went on to another workplace and repeated what she'd done at the dealership," Angie said. "It was nice of Jonas to want her to have another chance, but it seems her behavior at the non-profit wasn't a momentary lapse in Joelle's judgment. She has a problem and probably won't be able to stop stealing without help."

"The gambling problem is worrisome," the chief said. "If she's gambling her money away, she's probably stealing to fund her habit."

"Do you think it's possible that Joelle could be the intruder? Could she be the one who killed the officer and broke into all three women's homes?"

"I won't remove her from the suspect list. Joelle didn't get along with the women she worked with at Brighter Days, she seems to have strong feelings of animosity towards them, and she stole from Bev Tarant. So, yes, I think she could have done it."

With an expression of discomfort, Angie put both hands on her abdomen.

Chief Martin sat up and stared at her. "Is something wrong? Are you okay?"

"I'm okay. I've been having Braxton-Hicks contractions."

"Are you in labor?" the chief looked like he wanted to grab Angie and whisk her to the hospital.

"No, no. They're false contractions."

"How do you know?"

"Because nothing happens." Angie rubbed her baby bump. "They're just contractions and nothing ever advances. It's practice contractions."

"Are you sure?" The chief looked at her warily. "What if you're wrong?"

"Then I'll have the baby right here in the museum." When Angie saw the look on the chief's face, she added with a smile, "I'm kidding. I'm not going to have the baby yet."

The chief relaxed. "I was going to ask if you and Mr. Finch could come with me to Bev's house, but maybe it's not a good idea if you're feeling uncomfortable."

"I'm always feeling uncomfortable. It's perfectly fine. What do you want us to do?"

"Walk around in the house. See if you get any sensations from being there."

"I'm done with the bake shop for the day." Angie

stood up. "Let's go. I'll text Mr. Finch and see if he's available. We can swing by the Victorian and pick him up."

It turned out both Finch and Jenna were free and they all rode together to Bev Tarant's house. The chief led them through the garage and into the kitchen.

Jenna looked at the disarray in the room. A few things were on the floor ... a pair of scissors, a kitchen towel, a broken plate. A pot of African violets was overturned on the counter, a casualty of the dramatic fight that had gone on in the room.

"Bev Tarant must have fought like heck," Jenna said as she was about to lift up the flower pot. "Am I allowed to touch things in here? Can I right the violets?"

Chief Martin nodded. "The room's been processed. You can touch whatever you want to."

Jenna gave the flowers a drink of water and set the pot near the window.

Angie picked up the pieces of the broken plate and tossed them in the trash. "There's no reason to leave the things on the floor. When Bev comes back, the mess will trigger memories of the fight in her mind."

Chief Martin bent to pick up the scissors and the towel. "It will be hard enough for Bev to come back in here. No need to leave reminders of the fight all over the floor."

Finch ran his hand over the countertops. "Can you walk us through what happened? Did the entire interaction between Miss Tarant and the attacker happen in the kitchen?"

"Bev was in her bedroom, asleep, until the sound of the footsteps woke her up," the chief said. "The fight started in the hallway and went into the kitchen where most of the incident took place."

"Where is Miss Tarant's room?" Finch questioned.

The chief led the three people down the hall and into the bedroom. "This is the master bedroom. Bev woke up, and quietly slipped out of bed. She had pepper spray and a hammer on her bedside table."

Finch's eyebrows raised. "A hammer? My, my."

"Bev wasn't taking any chances," Jenna said. "She wanted access to a weapon in case the intruder broke into her home. It seems it came in handy."

"Good for her." Finch commended Bev's forethought and preparation.

The chief said, "Bev told us she stood in her room listening and when she heard more footsteps she lunged down the hall to meet the attacker. She didn't want to wait. She wanted to be the aggressor. Bev thought her behavior might throw off the intruder and give her an edge of surprise."

"It must have," Angie said. "He mustn't have been expecting Bev to come after him ... or *her*, if the attacker is a woman."

"I think I would have stood frozen in my room, if I had been in Bev's shoes," Jenna said. "I don't know if I could have mustered the courage to fight him."

"You would have, Miss Jenna," Finch said. "You wouldn't go down without a fight."

"Bev and the intruder met in the hall, probably right around there." The chief pointed to the spot. "They began to fight, and they ended up in the kitchen where the majority of the battle took place."

"What made the intruder leave?" Finch asked.

"Bev wasn't slowing down and she'd hit him with the hammer several times, probably causing injuries. The attacker must have thought it was time to get away," the chief surmised.

"And the intruder carried some things in a bag?" Finch asked.

"Weapons, rope, handcuffs, a stun gun."

Finch shook his head in disgust. "Shall we go back to the kitchen? I'd like to hold the things that were on the floor."

The plate shards were removed from the trash and set on the counter next to the scissors and the towel. Finch observed the items, then he picked up the shards, and closed his eyes for several minutes while Angie and Jenna walked from the kitchen, down the hall, and into the bedroom.

Next Finch took hold of the towel, repeating the process, and finally, he held the scissors in his hand. When his eyes popped open, he couldn't stifle a gasp.

"Mr. Finch?" the chief asked.

"I'm all right, Phillip. The sensations were so strong that they startled me."

Angie and Jenna returned to the kitchen to see Finch sitting on a stool at the kitchen island.

"Did you sense something, Mr. Finch?" Jenna asked.

"I did, indeed. I have no doubt in my mind that the person who trespassed here is the same person who left the bullet and the handcuffs on Bev's desk at work. I could feel the person's rage and his feelings of being rejected. He believes this is not the way his world is supposed to be, so he strikes out at those he feels are stifling his abilities and opportunities. He believes those people deserve to be punished."

Angie nodded. "I feel similar things that have been left behind in the house. Revenge and rage are floating on the air."

Jenna said, "So are competence and determination, and strength of will. Those things were left behind by Bev."

"As far as the attacker, does anyone pick up on a male energy as opposed to a female energy?" Angie asked.

Finch and Jenna thought about the question.

"I can't tell," Jenna said, a trace of disappointment in her voice.

"I keep picking up on a strong energy," Finch told them. "The energy is erratic and angry. I believe the person who broke into this house is the same one who broke into the non-profit. I also think this person will not abandon his objective until he reaches his goal."

"What's the objective?" the chief asked.

Finch clutched the top of his cane. "To murder Miss Bev Tarant."

21

When Angie and Chief Martin walked into Build Your Best Life gym, the people working out looked over at them without stopping what they were doing. The place was a wide open, high-ceilinged, industrial space with exercise balls, weights, and cardio equipment including rowing machines, stationary bikes, and treadmills.

The chief asked at the desk for the owner and a muscled, stocky man in his mid-forties came out to meet them.

"Stan Brookfield." The man's grip was strong and firm, and he led Angie and Chief Martin to a small office. "How can I help?"

"We'd like some information on one of your members, Joelle Young."

"Joelle's a hard worker, determined, resilient, keeps pushing until she achieves her goals. What do you want to know about her?"

"Does she come in often?"

"Six days a week. Without fail."

"When was she in last?"

Stan was about to say something, then stopped. "I didn't see her today. I don't think she was in yesterday either." The man stood up. "Let me go ask at the office."

In a minute, Stan was back. "Like I thought, Joelle hasn't been in for two days. That's very unusual. Someone in the office is giving her a call. I hope she isn't sick. Why are you asking about her?"

"There was an issue at a place she worked at. We wondered if you knew anything about it?" the chief asked.

"What was the issue?"

"You know that Joelle worked at Brighter Days? The non-profit?"

"Did you say *worked*? Doesn't she still work there?"

"No. She was let go," the chief informed the man.

"For what reason?"

"We aren't at liberty to say at the moment," Chief

Martin said. "Can you tell us about Joelle? Does she interact with the people here?"

"Joelle's kind of a loner," Stan said. "Nothing wrong with that. She isn't a big conversationalist. She does her thing. She'll talk when she's interested in something. Joelle doesn't believe in wasting energy, so if she hasn't got anything to say, she stays quiet. If she thinks you're boring or silly, she moves away from you and goes back to working out. She gets pleasure from pushing herself athletically. Her gains give her confidence."

"Does she get along with the people here? Has she had any trouble with anyone?"

Stan shook his head. "She gets along fine here. People know she might not respond if you talk to her. She gets into her workout and goes into her own world. There hasn't been any trouble with her."

A red-headed woman knocked on the door and stuck her head into the office. "Joelle doesn't answer her phone. It goes to voicemail. Lori is going to drive over to her place and knock on the door."

"Thanks," Stan told her, and the woman retreated.

"That's really nice that someone will go check on Joelle," Angie observed.

"We watch out for each other here," Stan said. "People become like a family."

"Do you know what Joelle likes to do when she's not working out?" the chief asked.

"She likes to go to the casino outside of Boston. She enjoys gambling," Stan told them. "Joelle isn't a problem gambler. She sets aside some money to play with and when it's gone, it's gone."

"Does she go to the casino often?" Angie asked.

"A couple of times a week, I think."

"Has anyone here ever accused Joelle of wrong-doing?" the chief questioned.

Stan's eyes widened. "Are you kidding me? Joelle doesn't do anything wrong. Are you sure you have the right person?"

"Does she talk about her family much?"

"Nah. Practically never. They live in Seattle, I believe. Joelle was in the military. Did you know that?" Stan asked.

"We do know that. She was in the Army, right?"

"Yes, she was. I think serving in the military added to her mental toughness. I also think it led to her being more of a loner. She doesn't talk about serving, but I bet she lost someone over there, a good friend, someone who was important to her. I think what she lost overseas has influenced her life.

Maybe she's afraid to lose someone again so she pulls inside of herself. Hey, I'm no psychologist. I'm just saying what I see."

The redhead came back. "Lori said no one answers the door at Joelle's. She said Joelle's car isn't in the driveway either. Maybe she went away for a few days."

"Thanks," Stan said to the woman before looking over at his guests. "That's weird. Joelle always tells one of us if she's going away. I didn't know anything about it."

"Maybe she's not away," Angie guessed. "Maybe she's out doing errands."

"I don't think so," Stan said. "Joelle wouldn't miss two days of workout unless she was deathly ill. Lori said the car isn't there. She must have left town for a few days. But, I'm telling you it's unusual. She tells someone here if she isn't going to be around. She tells the office people, at the very least."

It was dark outside when Angie and the chief left the gym and got into the police SUV.

"What do you think?" Angie asked.

"I think Joelle left town," the chief said. "Why she left town is the question."

"And she didn't tell anyone she was leaving,"

Angie pointed out. "Do you think it makes her look guilty?"

"The timing is interesting," the chief remarked. "Joelle didn't go to the gym on the day Bev was attacked and she didn't go there today. The man said it was unusual."

"Did she take off for a while because someone hit her with a hammer the other day?" Angie raised an eyebrow.

"It could be." Just when the chief started the engine, his phone buzzed and he looked at the message. He returned a text message before asking Angie, "Do you have time to take a ride over to Lydia Hendrick's place? She has something on her mind that she wants to speak with me about."

"Sure, I can."

"How are your fake contractions?" The chief eyed the young woman in the passenger seat.

"Gone. I'm fine now." Angie looked at the wintry scene outside of her window. "Do you know what Lydia has on her mind?"

"Not a clue. She wouldn't tell the officer, but she insisted that I get the message right away."

After parking in the driveway, Chief Martin and Angie rang the doorbell and were welcomed inside by Lydia.

"I'm so grateful you could come so quickly," the woman said.

"Is something wrong?" Angie asked.

"It seems so. I have an associate of Roger's here in the living room. I've asked him to tell you what he told me."

The associate stood up when Angie and the chief entered the living room and shook hands with them. Preston Wilkes was a partner at the same law firm where Roger worked. He was tall and slim and had silvery gray hair and blue eyes. He was dressed in a perfectly-tailored blue suit.

Everyone took seats.

"Preston came to see me out of concern," Lydia said. "I'm glad he did, even though it's made me very upset."

"What is it?" Angie asked.

Preston cleared his throat. "Roger has been off ever since the divorce with Lydia."

"Off, how?" the chief asked for clarification.

Preston waved his hand in the air. "Forgetful, foggy-brained, not as sharp as he usually is. He often seems fatigued, and then on other days, he's full of energy."

"Has his behavior worsened?"

"Somewhat, yes. I'd have to say, yes, it has."

Preston pushed his shoulders back. "He's been acting odd for the past couple of months. I've caught him babbling at his desk when he thinks he's alone. He seems aimless, disinterested in his work. He's been distant. He doesn't want to socialize, which is very unlike Roger."

"Do you know what caused him to worsen?" the chief asked.

"I don't know why, but I could venture a guess. He's in grief over his marriage. He's lost hope of ever getting back with Lydia. He seems to be spiraling into depression."

"Have you heard from Roger recently?" the chief asked Lydia.

"Yesterday, he texted. I hear from him every day or every other day."

"Did you respond to him?"

"I sent a brief response."

"Have you noticed a change in his behavior?" Chief Martin asked the woman.

"His texts and conversations seem as odd as they have for the past year. Slightly off-topic, tending to a rant, blaming me for every trouble he has."

"So no change, really?"

"Maybe a little more frantic," Lydia said. "What worried me was what Preston told me today."

"What was that?" the chief asked.

"I went into Roger's office the other day. Roger was sitting at his desk, hunched over something. I saw it was a small ragdoll, maybe six inches in length, maybe a little less. Roger got the doll on a business trip to South America last year. He kept it on a shelf in his office with other collectables." Preston shook his head. "Roger had a fountain pen in his hand and had the ragdoll on the table in front of him. He was stabbing the doll repeatedly. He said, 'I don't care. I just don't care.' Honestly, it was very unnerving behavior. I had to come and warn Lydia in case Roger ... well, you know."

"What do you mean? In case Roger does what?" Angie asked.

Looking very uncomfortable, Preston said, "In case Roger isn't in control of his faculties, and in case he decides to do something stupid that would ruin his life."

"Something stupid ... like kill me." Lydia's eyes darkened.

22

"Authorities tell me that Allen drove to Logan Airport in Boston early in the morning on the day you were attacked and he took a flight to Mexico," Chief Martin said to Bev Tarant. "Do you know if he's visited Mexico before?"

"I know he hasn't. I went one winter for two weeks and I told him about the historical sights there. Is it suspicious for him to have left the country?" Bev held her hands together in her lap.

"Not necessarily, but the timing is of interest."

"Allen didn't show any interest in going to Mexico when I was telling him about my experience there. In fact, he seemed against visiting. He said it was too hot and he didn't care for the heat."

The chief said, "It seems he's changed his mind."

Bev had taken a week off from work to recuperate from the attack and was staying at a friend's townhouse in Silver Cove. She had some cuts and purple bruises on her face and arms, and she had some muscle pain that made her walk with a limp.

"Has anything about the person who attacked you become clearer?" Angie asked.

"Really? No. Sometimes, I think it was Allen and sometimes I think it was Joelle, and then other times, I don't think I knew the person at all."

"Would you be open to hypnosis?" the chief asked.

"Hypnosis?" Bev had a look of surprise on her face. "That's a serious thing? For a crime investigation, I mean? Law enforcement uses that?"

"There are times when it has proven helpful. The findings can't be used in court, however."

"I don't know." Bev looked across the room at nothing. "Can I think about it for a few days?"

"Absolutely." The chief nodded.

"Have you heard that Joelle hasn't been at her gym for a couple of days?" Angie asked. "It's unusual for her to miss any training time. An employee of the gym drove over to Joelle's house and reported that no one came to the door and the car was missing from the driveway. The people at the gym told us that Joelle always tells them when she won't be in. We assume she left town, maybe she needed some time away."

"Isn't it odd that Joelle and Allen have left the area?" Bev said. "I don't think they're working together or anything like that, but it seems one of them must have fled because of the attack. Whoever broke into my house must not look so good right now, he'd have injuries from the hammer I hit him with. He or she might not want to show a damaged face to the world. It would certainly be suspicious if Joelle or Allen showed up with the physical signs of a fight. One of them must be guilty. What are the odds that both of them had a vacation planned for the same time? One of them must have fought with me in my house." Bev pushed at her hair. "Which one attacked me?"

"Does anything come into your mind when you think about being awoken the other morning?" the chief asked. "Some little thing? A movement, a sound, a scent? Anything that might point to Allen or Joelle?"

"When I think about it, I can clearly hear the squeak of the wood floor in the kitchen, and I can hear the sound of the person's foot taking a step. Remembering the sounds fill me with terror. I know there were grunts and moans when we were fighting, but I don't know which grunt came from me and which came from the intruder. It was a jumbled mess. There are parts of the experience that I can't even remember." Bev glanced out the window at the pretty snowy scene in the backyard. "I don't know if the attacker was a man or a woman because of the clothing and the mask. Joelle was in the Army and she works out all the time. Allen worked out, he ran, hiked. They were both strong. Joelle and Allen were similar in height. I can't think of anything that might differentiate one from the other since the attacker was wearing bulky clothes and a mask to hide the face."

"It's okay," the chief said. "If there's something that happened during the fight that can point to who broke into your house, one day, it will pop into your mind out of the blue."

"Do you think hypnosis would be a quicker way to bring things forward in my mind?" Bev asked.

"Sometimes, it is, but not always," the chief said. "If you're not comfortable with it, or not ready to do it, then don't push yourself."

"You're taking some time off from work?" Angie asked.

"Physically, I feel like I've been run over by a

bus," Bev said. "Mentally, I feel worse. I feel stressed, unsafe, distrustful, anxious. I don't have much of an appetite. I can't sleep at night. I'm afraid I'll wake up to an intruder. My friend is very kind and understanding and told me I can stay here as long as I want to. I'm grateful to her."

"Will you see a counselor? It might be helpful," Angie said encouragingly.

"I will. I have an appointment with someone later in the week. I figure it can't hurt to talk to someone. I'd like to get my life back to the way it was." Bev let out a sigh. "I wish none of this ever happened."

On the way to the next meeting, Chief Martin said, "I got a message while we were with Bev. It seems Joelle's phone isn't pinging from anywhere. It's either turned off or it's been destroyed."

"Maybe Joelle is someone who only turns her phone on when she needs to make a call," Angie suggested.

"Records indicate that Joelle's phone is usually on." The chief turned the police SUV onto a busy street.

"Maybe it got damaged and she's going to get a new one. It doesn't mean she's the intruder."

"No, but suddenly she goes off the grid? She didn't tell people at the gym that she wouldn't be in. She isn't at home. Her car is gone. Her phone is off. If she was employed, we could ask at the place of business if Joelle was at work, and if she wasn't, did she take vacation days. We could also ask if the time away was planned or unplanned. But since she got let go from her job, we don't have that avenue available to us."

"And what about Allen Poulin? Did you ask at his job if his time away was planned or not?"

"We did make an inquiry. I just got that information in a text a few minutes ago. Allen sent an email to his workplace manager and said he was taking a week off due to unexpected circumstances." The chief took a quick look at Angie with a raised eyebrow.

"Were the unexpected circumstances a fight in Bev Tarant's kitchen?" Angie asked.

"I'd love to know the answer to that." Chief Martin pulled the SUV into a parking spot and cut the engine.

Angie and the chief entered the building that housed the law firm where Roger Hendricks worked, and after riding up in the elevator and entering the elegant waiting room, they were ushered into the man's office.

Roger greeted them with firm handshakes and offered them seats.

"How can I help?" Roger asked. He gave the impression he was in control of himself and wasn't about to start stabbing a small South American ragdoll.

"Can you tell us if you've been in contact with Lydia recently?" the chief asked.

"I have. I'm not sure of the day, but it was recent."

"Did you talk to her about the intruder in her home?"

"Briefly. I don't think she wanted to talk much about it. What an awful thing. Lydia needs to get the house alarm fixed right away. Do you know if she's arranged that?"

"I'm not sure. Does Lydia think she knows the person who broke into her home?"

"She wouldn't tell me something like that. Lydia won't discuss anything personal with me."

"Did she say anything about the break-in to you? Sometimes, people subconsciously hold back when speaking with law enforcement. They often open up to family or friends."

Roger shook his head. "I wish she would tell me things. She is closemouthed with me. You'll have better luck checking with her friends."

The chief moved the topic of conversation to Roger and his well-being. "How have you been feeling?"

"Me? Besides feeling worried about Lydia, everything is going well."

"Have you come to terms with the ending of your marriage?" the chief asked.

"Not completely. I know I instigated the break-up with my behavior. I'm regretful about what I did. It was terrible judgment on my part, but I acted impulsively. I should have thought things through. I do wish Lydia would forgive me, but I don't think she has it in her."

Angie watched the man give his soliloquy and couldn't help feeling that he was only saying words, words he was supposed to say under the circumstances, but nothing came from his heart. *I wouldn't forgive him either.*

"Has the divorce impacted your ability to do your work?" Chief Martin asked.

"Not at all." Roger leaned forward. "Some of my colleagues worry about me. There isn't any need. I'm experiencing a life transition. Change can be hard, but ultimately, it will lead to new opportunities and newfound happiness."

"You have an excellent attitude." Angie wasn't sure if Roger had turned a corner in accepting the divorce or was articulately pulling their legs.

"I love Lydia and I always will. We've changed over the years and we've grown apart. It's time to take steps towards our new lives."

Chief Martin noticed the ragdoll on the shelf on the other side of the room. "Is that doll from South America?"

"It is. I picked it up on my travels there."

The chief stood up and walked over to have a closer look. "My wife likes things like this. She likes the local craftsmanship put into objects like this." The chief leaned closer. "The doll has been damaged? It seems to have some punctures in it."

Roger chuckled. "I've been using the doll as a stress-reliever. A couple of my colleagues thinks it's a childish way to deal with stress, but I've read articles that say it's best to let out your feelings of anger so they don't build-up internally."

"I see. Well, whatever works, I guess." The chief thanked the man for his time, and he and Angie left the office.

Once outside, Angie asked, "What did you think of Roger's explanation?"

"I think he's quick on his feet coming up with plausible responses. What do you think of him?"

"I pick up strong sensations of anger towards Lydia, but I can't tell if he'd do anything harmful to her or not. I get the feeling Roger doesn't know himself very well. He says things he thinks he should be saying. I think his inability to be in touch with his own feelings blocks me from being able to read him."

"The man makes me feel sad," the chief admitted. "He's like a walking, talking robot."

Angie thought that was a perfect way to describe Roger and his mechanical emotions.

23

Angie and Jenna sat at the round table in the jewelry studio staring at the screen of Angie's laptop. Euclid and Circe were curled on the sofa near the windows relaxing in the warm, late afternoon sunlight.

The sisters had spent the past thirty minutes doing an internet search on Allen Poulin. They'd found his educational background and his employment history, places he'd lived, and some social media posts and pictures showing him at college gatherings, sporting events, and parties.

"Wait a second." Angie leaned closer, her heart starting to pound. "It looks like Allen has been arrested twice."

"What?" Jenna's facial expression showed surprise. "What was he arrested for?"

"When he was eighteen, he was arrested for breaking and entering of a home in a wealthy suburb of San Francisco. He got community service hours to perform as his sentence. When he was twenty-two, he was arrested for assault on a woman. She claimed to be his friend and dropped the charges." Angie turned to her sister. "These are the things he got arrested for. How many other things did he do that he wasn't arrested for?"

"He's a bad apple." Jenna's brows furrowed. "He should have been given prison time for the assault, but a slap on the hand was all he got. He either intimidated the woman or he had a really good lawyer."

Angie said, "Chief Martin told me law enforcement has requested that border patrol alert the Sweet Cove and Silver Cove police departments if Allen Poulin attempts to cross the border and re-enter the country."

"Really? They're considering him a serious suspect."

"They want to know if he's back in the country so they can be on alert. He wants to be able to tell Lydia, Monica, and Bev if Allen's around, and to be on guard."

"What about Joelle? Is there any way they can

find out where she went and if she returns?" Jenna asked.

"Chief Martin has asked Joelle's gym to contact him when she returns to work out. They checked for her phone pinging and they've asked hospitals within a sixty-mile radius if she's been in for treatment. There aren't any reports of her being treated or admitted to a hospital."

"If Joelle is the one who broke into Bev's house, maybe she went out-of-state for treatment of injuries she sustained in the fight with Bev." Jenna fiddled with some gemstones that she'd been using to create a new necklace. "Who is the criminal? Who is the person who attacked a police officer, broke into the non-profit, and broke into the three women's homes. Why can't we sense more about what's going on?"

"Orla says most of our energy is going to the babies and there isn't much left for our paranormal skills to use. Mr. Finch thinks that Bev is the target."

"But three women were attacked, not just Bev," Jenna pointed out.

"Three *homes* were broken into." Angie paused. "*One woman* was attacked."

"Monica fought with the intruder in her house," Jenna said.

Angie said, "It seems to me that the intruder

didn't really fight with Monica. He or she made it seem like they were fighting. I think Bev is the real target. The intruder in *her* house planned to kill her. He brought in a bag with weapons, a stun gun, rope, handcuffs. He didn't bring those things into Lydia's or Monica's homes. He was using the other two women to throw off the police, to spread police protection thin, to create three targets in order to divide the attention and concern. I think Mr. Finch has been right all along. I think Bev is the one who has been in danger."

Euclid and Circe sat up and hissed.

Jenna sat blinking for several moments. "I think you're right. Do you think Joelle is hiding in plain sight, just waiting, biding her time for the right moment to strike again?"

"I think it's a real possibility."

"What about Allen? Did he really go to Mexico?"

"Border security says that he did," Angie said. "So he must have traveled there."

Jenna sat up. "Did Allen go there or did his passport go there? Did Allen give his passport to someone else? Did Allen pay someone to pretend to be him? Was it the imposter who traveled to Mexico?"

"Is Allen still here in the area?" Angie felt a wave

of fear rush through her body. "Is Allen waiting for the right moment to strike? Is he waiting for the right moment to kill Bev Tarant?"

Jenna said, "We need to speak to Chief Martin and share our ideas with him. He needs to tell Bev that the suspects might be right here in the area and that she needs to be on-guard."

"Who is it?" Angie asked. "Who is the person who's waiting like a venomous spider to take Bev's life?"

When Angie left the house to go to her doctor's appointment, the snow was coming down hard. She borrowed Jenna's car to drive the few miles to the office and was glad she'd left early because she had to drive slowly on the slippery roads.

Why is it always snowing? Angie sighed as she pulled into the parking lot of the medical offices and went inside to her appointment.

The doctor told her that it was probable that she would go into labor within the week. After hearing the news, Angie sat in the car for a few minutes thinking about meeting her daughter in a matter of days. Resting her hands on her baby bump, she closed her eyes and told Gigi she couldn't wait to meet her.

Brushing at her misty eyes, she started the car, excited to tell Josh the doctor's prediction. About to pull out of the lot, Angie checked to be sure no one was coming, and began to move the car into the street.

Suddenly, out of nowhere, a car sped forward at high speed and Angie jammed on the brakes. The slippery road and the sudden attempt to stop made the car start to slide, and she lifted her foot from the brake and gently turned the wheel to slow the skid.

The speeding car flew past very close to Angie's vehicle and missed her by only six inches.

Glaring out the window, Angie's blood boiled at the fool who nearly caused a collision. As she was about to drive into the street again, she paused and stared off at the dark blue car that was speeding away.

That driver.

Did she recognize the driver?

Was it?

Was it Allen Poulin?

24

When Angie rushed into the house through the backdoor, Courtney looked up from her spot at the kitchen island. "What's cookin'?"

"A lot. The doctor said I'd probably go into labor within the week and I think I saw Allen Poulin in town."

The cats sat up to attention on the refrigerator.

Courtney's face lit up. "Gigi will be here in a few days? I can't believe she'll really be here." The smile dropped from her face. "What did you say about Allen Poulin?"

Angie tossed her wool coat over one of the stools. "I think I saw him in town. He was speeding down the road. His car almost clipped mine. I had to jam on the brakes and I skidded partway into the street.

The driver looked like Allen, but I can't be sure it's him."

"I thought the authorities were going to alert Chief Martin if Allen returned to the country?" Courtney said. "The chief didn't tell us Allen was back so maybe it was someone who looked like him."

"Maybe. It's snowing hard so I couldn't see him clearly." Angie sank onto a stool. "What are you making? It looks good."

"I'm making two things. This is divinity. I'm putting in some different flavors of fruit jelly bits."

"Can I try some?"

Courtney handed her sister a square of divinity with pineapple bits and when Angie took a bite, she closed her eyes and moaned. "Delicious."

"I made some four-layer chocolate and caramel fudge, too. Try it." Courtney passed Angie a square of the fudge.

"Wonderful." Angie licked her finger. "I need more."

"Is it good for the baby?"

"A few bites of candy won't hurt anyone." Angie ate another small piece of fudge.

"I'm going to make tea." Courtney headed for the stove. "You want some?"

"Sure. No. I guess not." Angie rubbed at her forehead.

"Do you feel okay?" Courtney eyed her sister.

"Tired. A little headache." Angie went to get her bag and took out her phone. "I want to talk to Chief Martin." The call went to the chief's voicemail and she left a message.

"Are you worried?"

"I am. I feel antsy. I feel like something is wrong." Angie stood up and took her coat off the chair. "I'm going to go over to see Bev Tarant. I need to tell her what I saw."

"Can you call her?" Courtney asked.

"I don't have her number." Angie put on her coat. "I won't be long. I just want to tell Bev to be on the lookout just in case."

"Do you want me to come with you?"

"I'm okay."

The cats hissed and Angie looked up.

"It's no big deal," she told the felines. "I'm probably mistaken about Allen Poulin, but I feel like I have to give Bev a warning." Angie gave her sister a smile as she headed for the door. "Save some of that candy for when I get back."

When she heard the car leaving the driveway,

Courtney felt cold inside. "Maybe I should have gone with her."

Euclid threw back his head and howled.

With snow falling down around her, Angie rang the doorbell of the townhouse where Bev Tarant was staying. She rang it again when no one came to the door. Reluctantly, she started away down the granite steps when the door opened.

"Can I help you?" A woman with wet hair stood just inside the door wearing a bathrobe.

"I'm Angie Roseland. I've been working on the case of the intruder at Bev's home and workplace. Is Bev here?"

The woman at the door relaxed. "Bev went out. A friend talked her into going to a restaurant. We all thought it would do her good to be out for a while. She's been cooped up in here for several days. I have to be at a meeting in an hour or I would have joined them."

"Do you know where they went for dinner?" Angie questioned.

"Yeah. They went to Antonio's Italian restaurant in the next town over. Do you know it?"

Angie nodded. "I do. Thanks for your help."

"Is everything okay?" the woman asked with a tone of concern.

"I just wanted to see how Bev is doing." Angie hurried to her car as a strange sensation of alarm pulsed in her veins.

She drove to the next town, pulled into Antonio's lot, and walked to the door being careful not to slip on the snow collecting on the pavement.

A delicious smell of pasta, sauce, garlic, and onions floated on the air and made Angie's stomach growl as she told the hostess who she was looking for.

"Right this way." The hostess led her into one of the cozy dining rooms at the back of the restaurant.

Bev sat at a square table with an auburn-haired woman who looked to be about thirty-years old. Bev spotted Angie and waved her over.

"Hi. This is Lucy. She talked me into coming out for dinner." Bev still had black and blue bruises on her face and hands, but she looked lighter and happier. "I was glad to get out of the house for a while. Sit with us."

Angie introduced herself to Bev's companion and took a seat. "I don't want to interrupt you. I'll just stay for a minute."

There was a bottle of wine on the table. Lucy said, "I'd offer you a glass, but I see you're expecting so you mustn't be drinking."

"You're right. I'm not, but thanks." Angie felt like she'd swallowed a bottle of jumping beans. Her body pulsed with anxiety and nervousness.

"Are you meeting your husband for dinner here?" Bev asked.

"What?" Angie felt foggy in the head. "Oh, no. I'm not."

"Did you come to pick up some takeout?" Lucy questioned.

"No." Angie made eye contact with Bev.

Bev's facial muscles tightened. "Is something wrong?"

"Listen. I'm probably mistaken, but I thought I saw Allen Poulin driving past me in Sweet Cove." Angie's voice shook a little.

"What? Allen is back?" Bev's hand trembled. "Chief Martin didn't tell me." The woman glanced around the restaurant. "He's back in the country?"

"I could be wrong about seeing him, but I wanted to tell you just in case."

"Did the authorities alert Chief Martin?" Bev looked like she would bolt from her chair.

"I don't know."

"Where did you see Allen?" Bev's eyes were like lasers.

Angie told her what had happened when she was leaving her doctor's office. "I only got a quick look at the driver."

"Maybe I'd better go home." Bev looked at her friend. "Why don't we ask the waiter to box up the dinners for us? We can eat at the townhouse. I don't feel comfortable being out in public if Allen is on the loose. Until we know for sure one way or the other if Allen is back or not, I'd like to stay at the townhouse."

"That's fine with me. We can light a fire in the fireplace," Lucy said. "It will be cozy."

"I'm going to go to the bathroom first." Bev got up and walked quickly out of the dining room.

Angie and Lucy chatted.

"When are you due?" Lucy asked.

Angie felt a painful twang in her abdomen. "In about a week, but babies seem to have a mind of their own and come when they're ready."

"A lot of babies are late. You'll probably go a little past your due date," Lucy told her. "It's pretty common."

Angie heard a scuffle in the hall that led to their dining room and her head turned. When she heard shouts, she leapt to her feet and grabbed a knife from the table, then darted to the hallway.

Bev was standing in the hall clutching her side. "How did you get back without anyone knowing about it?"

Looking wild-eyed and disheveled, Allen Poulin stood a foot in front of Bev wielding a long blade knife ... he lunged at her and knocked the young woman to the floor where he began to stab her.

Bev screamed.

Angie ran forward and hit Allen in the back with the small knife she'd taken from the table. He reached for her leg and yanked her to the ground.

Angie slashed at Allen's hand, but he pushed at her and turned back to stab Bev.

Leaning to the side, Angie jabbed the small blade into Allen's arm.

Infuriated, Allen turned on her, but before he could strike Angie with his knife, a patron from the dining room ran into the hall and wrestled Allen into a hold.

More patrons ran forward to help and pinned Allen to the floor, kicking the blade from his hand.

Angie crawled to Bev. The young women lay flat on her back, blood coming from the wounds on her arms, chest, and neck.

Her eyes fluttered open and she reached for Angie's hand. "Thanks for saving me." Bev's voice was hoarse. "I don't feel so good." The grip she had on Angie's hand went limp.

"Bev. Bev." Angie touched the young woman's cheek. "Help's coming. Stay here with me. Do you hear me, Bev?"

Someone knelt beside the two women and checked Bev's pulse. "It's faint, but her heart is still beating."

Angie felt a contraction and she bent forward.

The person next to her noticed. "I'll help you up."

Shaking her head, Angie said, "No, I'm staying with Bev." Tears fell from her eyes and dropped onto the young woman's forehead.

Allen ranted and squirmed while the patrons held him down.

"I don't deserve to live," Allen screamed over and over.

Angie gently stroked Bev's face and whispered, "I'm right here. I won't leave you. It's okay now, you're safe. He can't hurt you. He won't ever hurt you again."

When another contraction came, Angie

breathed deeply and slowly. She put one hand on her belly, the other hand held onto Bev's.

Not now, sweet Gigi. Give me just a little while longer.

Feeling a tender touch on her back, Angie looked around to see Josh and Courtney standing over her.

"We're a little late, sis, but we're here now." Courtney knelt beside her sister and Josh wrapped his wife in his arms.

And Angie burst into tears.

25

"Where's Jenna?" Angie asked from the backseat of the car.

"She's at the Victorian. Her labor started about two hours ago," Courtney said.

"Who's with her?"

"Mr. Finch and Ellie, and Euclid and Circe, and Tom is on his way there."

"Why did you come to the restaurant?"

"Right after you left, I started to feel like something was wrong. The fact that the cats were acting crazy and howling non-stop was also a clue that something was up," Courtney deadpanned. "I called Josh and he met me at Bev's friend's townhouse. She was just leaving. She told me where you went."

"I want to go home," Angie said as another contraction came on. "I want to be with everyone."

"We're going to the hospital," Courtney told her.

Josh was driving and the snow was coming down so hard, he could barely see a foot in front of him. "I don't know if we're going to make it to the hospital. The snow is piling up. I think we better turn around. The Victorian is closer than the hospital."

"Good," Angie said clutching her baby bump. "I want to go home."

Josh looked in the rearview mirror at Courtney sitting beside Angie with her arm around her sister. "What do you think?"

Courtney let out a long breath. "Let's turn around."

"You know all about delivering babies." Angie forced a smile. "You read about it in that book."

"Yes, I did, so we're all set." Courtney added, "There's also an obstetrician staying at the bed and breakfast in case I'm not the best at actually delivering a baby."

Angie grimaced as another contraction took hold. "I get the feeling that Gigi isn't going to need much help being born."

"Hang on," Josh warned as the car slipped and slid over the road when he took a turn. He leaned forward trying to see the road through the driving snow and he gripped the wheel so tightly that his knuckles went white. "We're almost home. Just a little further."

Courtney blew a sigh of relief when Josh pulled the car, slipping and sliding, into the driveway and came to a slow stop in front of the carriage house.

With a coat tossed over her shoulders, Ellie darted out to meet them and yanked open the rear door of the car. "How is she?"

"They took Bev to the hospital," Courtney told her. "She didn't look good."

"I hope Bev makes it, but I meant Angie. How is she?" Ellie got in beside her sister. "Can you walk, Angie? Do you need to be carried? Tom's inside and we can get a few of the guests to help."

"Is Jenna here?" Angie managed to ask.

Ellie gave Courtney a look.

"What is it?" Courtney demanded. "Why are you looking at me like that?"

"Jenna's contractions are coming fast," Ellie said. She put her hand on Angie's shoulder. "Let's get you into the house."

Josh leaned down to look into the backseat. "I can lift you out."

"I can do it." Angie sat up and scrooched her butt

over the car seat to the door. "Take my hand, Josh, so I don't fall."

Josh took one side and Ellie took the other, and they carefully and slowly ushered Angie over the snowy walkway and into the house where they helped her upstairs, pausing for a few minutes in the middle of the staircase for her to manage a contraction.

Euclid and Circe had been standing in the back hall watching for Angie's arrival and when she came inside, they trilled to her, and followed behind her every step of the way.

Tom was at the top of the stairs. "Do you need me?"

"I'm okay, thanks," Angie said. "Where's Jenna?"

"She's here in the spare bedroom. It's too dangerous to try and get to the hospital."

"I want to see her." Angie walked gingerly into the room to find her twin sister sitting on the edge of the bed with Mr. Finch sitting beside her.

"Hello, Miss Angie." Finch got up to hug the young woman. "We're all here. Everything is going to be fine. The obstetrician is ready and willing to help, should you or Jenna need or want her."

"Thanks, Mr. Finch."

Jenna's faced looked tired, but she gave Angie a

smile. "We continue to do everything together. These two kids are really going to be like twins."

With Finch's help, Angie sank down next to Jenna. "Want to race?" she asked.

Jenna chuckled. "I think I might be ahead of you in labor, so yes, I'll take the challenge. There's another twin bed in here so why don't you join me?"

"Glad to."

Josh helped Angie to the other bed, and she rested on her side for several minutes waiting for the next contraction. When it came, she breathed in and out slowly with Josh holding her hand, ready to coach her as the contractions progressed.

Euclid and Circe sat on the dresser to keep watch.

"I thought first babies took forever to be born," Courtney said.

"They do, except in these two cases." Ellie brought in some clean towels and two cool cloths for the sisters' foreheads.

Occasionally, Angie or Jenna would get up to walk around the room a little and offer encouragement to each other. Josh and Tom brought in rocking chairs and placed them next to their wives' beds so they could sit close to them. Mr. Finch sat in the easy chair in the corner texting Ellie and

Courtney whenever anything was needed so they could hurry up the stairs with the requested items.

Tom looked out the window. "Look at the snow coming down. The forecast didn't predict this. There'll be two feet out there when it's over."

"And when it's over," Josh smiled at his brother-in-law, "we'll both be dads."

Jenna squeezed her husband's hand as she meandered past his rocker, and Tom's eyes misted over. "I can't wait," he said. "Need anything, hon?"

Jenna kissed him on the top of his head. "I'm good."

After two hours passed, Angie's and Jenna's contractions were coming very close together, and suddenly, the two cats howled at the same time.

Angie's breath caught in her throat, and she told Josh, "I have to push."

Finch texted Ellie and Courtney and they flew up the stairs carrying washcloths, diapers, and baby blankets.

Mr. Finch touched Angie's forehead, and when the look of pain on her face washed away, he headed for the door to give her and Josh some privacy.

"Don't leave," Angie told the man as she pushed.

"Stay with us, Mr. Finch," Josh said with a nod, and the older man returned to his seat pleased that the family wanted him to be there when Gigi was born.

Ellie moved a stool to the end of the bed and prepared to deliver the infant. "The baby's head is crowning."

Holding Angie's hand, Josh was so excited and emotional that he looked shaky and weak and Courtney kept her eye on him in case he was about to go down.

"Push again," Ellie told her sister. "A couple of more good pushes are all you need."

A minute later, the baby made her appearance with a strong, loud cry, a cough, and a sneeze.

The cats trilled triumphantly as Ellie handed the little girl to her mother.

Tears streamed down Josh's face as he welcomed his daughter to the world and Angie stroked the baby's cheek.

"Sweet Gigi. I've been waiting a very long time to meet you."

Jenna's breathing changed and Ellie hurried to the end of her other sister's bed.

"Your baby's coming. Push, Jenna," Ellie said with encouragement.

Finch rose and went to Jenna's side where he

touched her forehead, and the touch seemed to ease Jenna's discomfort.

In minutes, another baby's cry filled the air, and everyone in the room with Jenna cheered.

"It's a girl!" Ellie exclaimed, and handed the little one to Jenna.

It was Tom's turn to cry now, and he blubbered as he stroked Jenna's hair and put his big hand tenderly on his daughter's back. "Welcome to the world, Libby."

"Two girls," Courtney hooted. "Just like when Angie and Jenna were born. Wait." She looked at Tom and Jenna. "Did you say Libby?"

Jenna smiled as she hugged the tiny, new infant. "Her name is Elizabeth Faith. Elizabeth after Mom, and Faith after Tom's mother."

"We're going to call her Libby." Tom beamed a wide smile.

"I love it," Courtney said. "Libby and Gigi."

After cooing over the children, Courtney, Ellie, and Mr. Finch left the room so the couples and their new daughters could spend time together. Of course, the two fine felines stayed in the room to keep watch over the newest additions to the family.

"What a happy day." Finch's smile lit up the second floor hallway. "I don't think there's ever been a happier day in my entire life." He, Courtney, and Ellie stood together with their arms around one another.

"I can't believe they're finally here," Courtney wiped at tears of joy. "You were great," she told Ellie. "Maybe you should give up running the bed and breakfast and become a midwife."

"No way. That was enough stress and excitement for me. I almost passed out a couple of times." When Ellie pushed her hair from her forehead, her hand visibly trembled.

"You never showed it, Miss Ellie." Mr. Finch had been amazed at her calm and competent manner.

"I'm a good actress." Ellie's face was white. "Now take me downstairs and make me a cup of tea before I collapse."

They walked down the wide carved staircase three-abreast, with arms linked, and Courtney holding tight to the railing with one hand. Suddenly, she stopped and took a glance at Mr. Finch.

"You touched Angie's and Jenna's foreheads when they were about to push," Courtney noted. "What was that about? They seemed so relaxed and serene after you touched them."

"I don't know what you mean," Finch said with his eyes twinkling. "I didn't do anything at all."

26

Angie and Jenna were cuddling with the babies in the family room when Chief Martin and Lucille came by with some gifts for the little girls. Lucille cooed over the babies and asked about the deliveries.

The cats were on the opposite sofa keeping an eye on their new responsibilities.

"I see Euclid and Circe are ever vigil when it comes to Gigi and Libby," the chief said.

"They're like guard dogs," Jenna smiled, and then modified her comment, "I mean guard cats. They even come to our house every day to check on Libby if we haven't come by the Victorian."

"I don't think they like that you and Tom and Libby don't live here," Angie said.

"We're only two doors down," Jenna chuckled.

Ellie, Courtney, and Mr. Finch came in carrying trays with tea and desserts and they set everything out on the big coffee table.

"Tell us the news," Angie said to the chief. "How is Bev?"

Bev Tarant had been stabbed eleven times by Allen Poulin. She was taken to the hospital and after surgery, was listed in critical condition with the medical staff not hopeful for a recovery. After several days, Bev surprised the doctors by rallying and her condition had been upgraded.

"Bev is expected to live," the chief said. "She's responding well to treatment and the doctors believe she will eventually make a full recovery. There's a long road to travel first, with more surgery and physical therapy, but it's truly amazing that Bev didn't succumb to her injuries."

"I'm so very glad," Angie said.

"Witnesses at the restaurant reported that Bev fought back when Allen attacked her in the hall with the knife. This was before you came to her aid. Bev had already been stabbed twice prior to you arriving in the hall. If you hadn't run out to help her, the doctors are sure Bev wouldn't have survived."

"I'm grateful to the other patrons who ran to help." Angie looked down at the sleeping baby in her arms. "If they hadn't helped, Bev and I probably would have been killed." She knew if she'd died, then Gigi probably wouldn't have survived either, but Angie just couldn't say those words aloud.

"I'd like to go see Bev when she's able to have visitors," Angie said. "Maybe I can bring Gigi."

"She told me she'd love to have you visit when she's feeling up to it," the chief said. "She's beyond grateful to you."

"What about Allen?" Ellie's eyes were hard.

"Allen has been arrested for the murder of a police officer and for the attempted murder of Bev Tarant, along with a good many other charges," Chief Martin said. "Border security dropped the ball when Allen went through customs. They were supposed to report the man's arrival in the country to law enforcement, but they didn't do it. An investigation will be conducted into where the breakdown in communication occurred."

"So what was Allen's rage all about?" Courtney asked.

"Allen was infuriated when Bev wanted to stop dating him. He has some serious mental issues. He's been in trouble with the law before for assault and for breaking and entering. A journal was found at Allen's place. He wrote about how he was in love with Bev and how she didn't deserve to live for rejecting him. He plotted the break-ins at the non-profit. The purpose was to frighten Bev. He wanted to make police think that there was more than one target, but Bev was his intended victim."

"Did Mr. Poulin write in his journal about why he broke into the other women's homes?" Finch asked.

"It was a tactic to keep law enforcement concerned about three targets, to spread us thin, to try and make Bev think someone other than herself was the real target thereby lowering her guard."

Jenna said, "Allen broke into Monica's and Lydia's homes, but he didn't have any plan to kill them. It was all intended to throw off the police. Angie thought this was what was going on. We talked about it right before Bev was attacked in the restaurant."

"Allen broke into Bev's home intending to murder her," the chief said. "Bev fought back in a way that surprised Allen. He never expected the level of intensity that he met when he attacked her. This information was written in his journal."

"I saw Allen the day he attacked Bev at the restaurant," Angie said. "He almost caused a collision with me when I was leaving the doctor's office. It was an incredible coincidence for me to see him as he went past. I felt antsy and anxious after that, and decided I had to warn Bev that Allen might be back."

"It's a lucky thing for Bev that you showed up at that restaurant," the chief acknowledged. "The stars aligned and brought good luck."

"What about Joelle Young? She was a suspect, especially when she disappeared from town and no one knew where she was," Courtney said. "Has she been located?"

"Joelle returned to town on her own," the chief reported. "She had gone to Boston for a job interview and stayed a few nights in the city to meet with a counselor. Joelle wants to beat her gambling habit and knows she needs help to do it. She got the job, by the way, and is very happy about it. She found an apartment near a gym and will be moving there in a week. She's also set up weekly meetings with the counselor. She told me that she's mentally tough when it comes to working out and athletics and she wants to apply that strength to managing her gambling problem."

"Good for her," Angie smiled. "I'm glad that

Joelle is making some changes that will lead to a healthier, happier life."

The group enjoyed desserts and talked about other things besides murder and criminals. The weather had taken a surprising and welcome turn bringing sunny skies and not a flake of snow for the past eight days. They all knew the snow and cold would return, but the break from the winter weather had lifted their spirits and cheered them.

When the chief and Lucille left, Ellie, Finch, and Courtney sat for a few minutes longer in the family room before heading off to their rooms.

Jenna said, "Everything's been such a whirlwind, I haven't told you something. Nana was in the room when we were delivering. I saw her standing over near Mr. Finch. She looked so happy. I think Nana will be around a lot more now that Libby and Gigi are here."

"I bet she will," Finch said with a nod.

"Thanks to all of you for helping us deliver the babies," Angie said to the family members. "Having you with us made the experience calm and relaxed. We felt loved and safe and cared for."

"It was the best," Jenna beamed. "You took such good care of me and Angie. It wouldn't have been the same without you with us."

"It was one of the best days of my life," Finch said dabbing at his eyes. "But I think with these two sweet additions to the family, the best is yet to come."

An hour later, Josh and Tom came home and sat with their wives and daughters in front of the fire in the family room. Euclid and Circe were curled on the rug near the fireplace.

"We're parents." Tom's face was full of joy as he looked down at little Libby in his arms.

"And we'll never have a full night's sleep again," Angie kidded.

"But it's worth it." Josh held Gigi close to his chest.

Jenna and Tom bundled up their little one to head home, and the foursome shared hugs as they walked to the door.

"See you tomorrow," Angie told her sister and brother-in-law.

Josh locked the door, and then he put his arm around Angie as they headed to the stairs to go up to their suite for the night.

"Mr. Finch said he thinks the best part of our lives is yet to come," Angie told her husband.

"Mr. Finch is a wise man," Josh smiled.

The new family of three started up the stairs

together in the big, beautiful, cozy house with the two fine felines following behind ... surrounded by family and love, and with hearts full of hope for happy days and peaceful nights.

THANK YOU FOR READING! RECIPES BELOW!

Books by J.A. WHITING can be found here:
www.amazon.com/author/jawhiting

To hear about new books and book sales, please sign up for my mailing list at:
www.jawhiting.com

Your email will never be sold, shared, or spammed.

If you enjoyed the book, please consider leaving a review. A few words are all that's needed. It would be very much appreciated.

ABOUT THE AUTHOR

J.A. Whiting lives with her family in New England. Whiting loves reading and writing mystery stories.

Visit me at:

www.jawhiting.com

www.bookbub.com/authors/j-a-whiting

www.amazon.com/author/jawhiting

www.facebook.com/jawhitingauthor

SOME RECIPES FROM THE SWEET COVE SERIES

Recipes

STRAWBERRY SCONES

INGREDIENTS FOR SCONES

2⅓ cups of all-purpose flour

2 Tablespoons granulated sugar

1 Tablespoon baking powder

¼ teaspoon salt

1 stick unsalted butter

1¼ cup chopped fresh strawberries

2 eggs

½ cup heavy whipping cream

1 Tablespoon of milk (to brush the top of the scone)

⅓ to ½ Tablespoon sugar (to sprinkle on top of the scone)

INGREDIENTS FOR GLAZE

⅔ cup of confectioner's sugar

1 Tablespoon of milk

DIRECTIONS FOR SCONES

Set oven to 400°F.

Using a large mixing bowl, mix together flour, sugar, baking powder, and salt.

Add the stick of butter (diced) and cut it into the flour mixture until it looks like coarse crumbs, about the size of peas.

Gently mix in the fresh strawberries.

Create an indentation in the center of the mixture; set aside the bowl.

In a smaller mixing bowl, lightly beat two eggs.

Stir in the heavy whipping cream.

Add the egg mixture to the flour mixture.

Use a spoon to stir the mixture until moist (be careful not to over mix).

Place the dough onto a floured sheet of parchment paper.

Shape the dough into a circle about ¾ inch thick.

Cut into 12 wedges; move the wedges apart (½ inch apart or slightly more).

Brush the wedges with the 1 Tablespoon milk and sprinkle with sugar.

Bake at 400°F for 15 minutes, or until lightly golden.

DIRECTIONS FOR GLAZE

Stir together confectioner's sugar and 1 Tablespoon of milk.

If you need to thicken the glaze, add a little more confectioner's sugar; if you need to make it thinner, add a little more milk.

Drizzle the glaze over the scones (after they have baked).

Scones can be served warm or at room temperature.

Store covered in the refrigerator; you may heat them up in a microwave for about 10 seconds.

GREEK BUTTER COOKIES

INGREDIENTS

1 cup butter, softened

¾ cup sugar

1 egg

¾ teaspoon vanilla extract

¾ teaspoon almond extract

2¼ cups all-purpose flour

½ cup of confectioner's sugar (to roll the cookies in)

DIRECTIONS

Set the oven to 400°F.

Grease cookie sheets.

In a medium mixing bowl, cream together butter, sugar, and egg.

Stir in the vanilla and almond extracts.

Blend in the flour; you may need to knead by hand to form the dough.

Use a teaspoonful of dough at a time to roll into a ball (form into "S" shape in you prefer).

Place cookies on the greased cookie sheets, about 1-2 inches apart.

Bake for 10 minutes, or until lightly golden and firm.

Cool completely.

Gently roll the cookies in the confectioner's sugar.

FASOLAKIA (GREEK STYLE GREEN BEANS AND POTATOES)

INGREDIENTS

2 bags of frozen green beans (about 8 cups total)

3 Yukon Gold potatoes, cut into small pieces (½ – ¾ inches)

1 14-ounce can or carton of diced tomatoes

3⅓ Tablespoons tomato paste

⅓ cup olive oil

½ cup water

1 yellow onion

4 cloves garlic

1 Tablespoon dried oregano

Salt and pepper to personal taste

Feta cheese (for serving)

DIRECTIONS

Peel and grate the onion (use a cheese grater).

Dice the potatoes.

Mince the garlic.

Add ¼ cup of olive oil to large pot and heat to medium-high.

Add the onion and the garlic to the olive oil and sauté for 5-6 minutes.

Add oregano and salt and pepper and sauté for 1 minute.

Add tomatoes, tomato paste, green beans, potatoes, water, and the rest of the olive oil; mix well.

Reduce the heat and let the mixture come to a high-simmer, covered, for about 30 minutes; stir frequently to prevent burning.

After 30 minutes or when the green beans and potatoes are tender, remove the lid and simmer 15-20 minutes more; stir often to prevent burning.

Add salt and pepper to taste.

Serve with feta cheese and some crusty bread or pita bread.

CHOCOLATE CARAMEL FOUR-LAYER FUDGE

INGREDIENTS FOR BOTTOM LAYER

1¼ chocolate chips cups

⅓ cup butterscotch chips

⅓ cup creamy peanut butter

INGREDIENTS FOR SECOND LAYER

¼ cup butter

¾ cup sugar

¼ cup evaporated milk

1½ cups marshmallow (like Fluff)

⅓ cup creamy peanut butter

1¼ teaspoon vanilla extract

INGREDIENTS FOR CARAMEL LAYER (3rd LAYER)

1 package (about 14 ounces) of individually wrapped caramels – unwrap them

⅓ cup heavy cream

INGREDIENTS FOR TOP LAYER (4th LAYER)

1 cup chocolate chips

⅓ cup butterscotch chips

⅓ cup creamy peanut butter

DIRECTIONS FOR BOTTOM LAYER

Grease a 9x13" dish.

In a small sauce pan combine chocolate chips, butterscotch chips, and creamy peanut butter using low heat.

Heat and stir until melted together with a smooth consistency.

Spread over the bottom of the pan.

Refrigerate.

DIRECTIONS FOR SECOND LAYER

In a saucepan over medium-high heat, melt the butter.

Stir in the sugar and the evaporated milk.

Bring to a boil – let the mixture gently boil for about 4 minutes.

Remove from the heat.

Stir in the marshmallow (Fluff), peanut butter, and vanilla.

Spread over the bottom layer.

Refrigerate until set.

DIRECTIONS FOR THIRD LAYER

In a saucepan over low heat, combine caramels and cream.

Heat and stir until the mixture is melted and has a smooth consistency.

Spread over the filling.

Refrigerate until set.

DIRECTIONS FOR TOP LAYER (4th LAYER)

In a saucepan over low heat, combine chocolate chips, butterscotch chips, and peanut butter.

Heat and stir until melted and the mixture has a smooth consistency.

Spread over the caramel layer.

Chill for about an hour.

Cut into 1-inch squares.

ENJOY!